Jena laughed

Then he stretched [...] ders, and she knew he wasn't just being overfriendly anymore.

She closed her eyes. "Travis, what are you doing?" When no reply came forth, she turned to look at him.

He met her questioning stare. "I'm falling for my summer girl, that's what I'm doing."

Jena glanced down at her hands, gripping the novel in her lap. She could scarcely believe the words Travis spoke—like something out of a beautiful love story.

"The truth is," he said, leaning closer, "I've been falling for you for months."

Her heart seemed to swell in her chest.

"Jena, say something, will you?"

"I can't. I think I just forgot how to breathe."

ANDREA BOESHAAR was born and raised in Milwaukee, Wisconsin. Married for twenty years, she and her husband Daniel have three adult sons. Andrea has been writing for over thirteen years, but writing exclusively for the Christian market for six. Writing is something she loves to share, as well as, help others develop. Andrea quit her job to stay home, take care of her family, and write.

HEARTSONG PRESENTS

Books under the pen name Andrea Shaar
HP79—An Unwilling Warrior

Books by Andrea Boeshaar
HP188—An Uncertain Heart
HP238—Annie's Song
HP270—Promise Me Forever
HP279—An Unexpected Love
HP301—Second Time Around
HP342—The Haven of Rest
HP359—An Undaunted Faith
HP381—Southern Sympathies
HP401—Castle in the Clouds
HP428—An Unmasked Heart
HP466—Risa's Rainbow

The Summer Girl

Andrea Boeshaar

Heartsong Presents

To my former neighbors and precious friends who resided on
the 3900 block of Prospect Avenue in Shorewood, Wisconsin,
from 1965 to 1975. Ours was a closely-knit neighborhood
made famous by its Fourth of July block parties and Mr.
Sheldon's motorcycle rides up and down the street. The mem-
ories I have of you all will remain near and dear to my heart.

A special hello to Patty Andrews. I hope you don't mind
that I moved my characters into your childhood home. . .and
then remodeled it!

A note from the Author:
I love to hear from my readers! You may correspond
with me by writing:

Andrea Boeshaar
Author Relations
PO Box 719
Uhrichsville, OH 44683

ISBN 1-58660-691-3

THE SUMMER GIRL

All Scripture quotations, unless otherwise indicated, are taken from
the HOLY BIBLE, NEW INTERNATIONAL VERSION ®. NIV®. Copyright ©
1973, 1978, 1984 by International Bible Society. Used by permission
of Zondervan Publishing House. All rights reserved.

All of the characters and events in this book are fictitious. Any
resemblance to actual persons, living or dead, or to actual events is
purely coincidental.

PRINTED IN THE U.S.A.

one

Needs a "Summer Girl." Jena Calhoun glanced at the piece of paper Mrs. Barlow handed to her at church yesterday, then looked back up at the Spanish-looking house looming in front of her. According to Mrs. Barlow, the owner and occupant of this place, a lawyer by the name of Travis Larson, would be expecting Jena.

"You'll be perfect for the position," insisted old Mrs. Barlow who lived next door to the Larsons. "Travis's daughters will adore you, and the job will solve all your problems."

Yes, it sure would, Jena thought as she neared her destination. Located on the corner of Prospect Avenue and Shorewood Boulevard, the two-story hacienda had a white stucco exterior with a red tile roof. It looked like it belonged in Mexico, not in this small suburb of Milwaukee, Wisconsin. A tall, redwood fence surrounded a tiny courtyard, and a narrow roof above the back door joined the house to a little apartment that sat above the two-car garage.

Jena made her way up the front steps, her palms sweating and her stomach filled with perpetual flutters. She hadn't ever been good at impressing others. She only knew how to be herself: Jennifer Ann Calhoun—Jena, for short.

But would that be enough to get her the job?

Lord, I need Your help. . .

Taking a deep breath, she pressed on the doorbell. Within a minute, the door swung open, and she found herself looking up into the face of a very handsome man with a very stern countenance.

"Yes?"

"Hello," she began, smiling politely, "I'm Jena Calhoun, and I'm here to interview for the summer girl position."

The dark-headed man's expression changed from severe to surprise. "You? You're Jena?"

"Why, yes. Is there a problem?"

"Well, no. . ." The man opened the door a bit wider and beckoned her inside. "I was just expecting someone a little younger—like, fifteen years old."

"Oh?"

The man indulged her with a smile, patronizing as it seemed. "Usually summer girls are teenagers," he explained. "I was expecting a fifteen-year-old."

"I see." Jena chewed her lower lip in contemplation. Her friend, Mary Star, had given her a lift to Mayfair Mall, a popular shopping center on Milwaukee's west side. From there, Jena had taken two city buses to get here to the small village of Shorewood, a suburb on the shores of Lake Michigan. It seemed such a shame that now she wouldn't even get an interview. "Well," she said at last, "thanks anyway."

She had turned to leave when the man grabbed her elbow. "Whoa! Where you going?"

Jena swung around and looked at him, taking note of his frown and the concern in his chocolate-brown eyes. "I'm twenty-six. I guess I'm too old to be a summer girl."

The man chuckled. "Perhaps, but let's talk anyway." He guided her into the well-lit living room. Six tall white wood-framed windows graced the entire front wall. A sofa and matching love seat, upholstered in greens and mauves against an ivory background, had been expertly placed on plush, cream colored carpeting. Jena wondered if the man was going to ask her to slip out of her shoes before she walked on the immaculate wall-to-wall rug.

He didn't.

"Come in, please, and sit down. Maybe I'll redefine the summer girl position and interview you as a possible nanny." He grinned.

Jena, however, wondered if she'd just been insulted. She thought the title of "nanny" sounded so...subservient. She sat down on the sofa anyway as the man took a place on the love seat across from her.

"So you're the girl. . .I mean the woman Mrs. Barlow recommended."

"Yes, I guess I am."

"Hmm. . ." The man appeared thoughtful. "Mrs. Barlow kept referring to you as 'such a sweet girl,' so, obviously, I pictured a girl."

"Sorry." Jena didn't know what else to say, and she was beginning to regret even coming here.

"Oh, no need for apologies." Travis cleared his throat. "I understand you and Mrs. Barlow attend the same church."

"Yes, that's right."

"In Menomonee Falls."

Jena nodded.

"You know," he began with a puzzled frown, "I never did figure out why Mrs. Barlow went all the way out there just for church when there's one not even a mile away from here."

"Her son's family lives in the Falls," Jena told him, "so she spends Sundays with them, and of course, she's a proud grandmother."

"Oh, right. I forgot about her son and his family." The man rubbed his palms together. "Well, enough chitchat, let's get down to business. I'll tell you about the job. I have two daughters, Mandi and Carly. Mandi is six and Carly is three. My sister has cared for them since my wife died, shortly after Carly's birth. But then Glenda, my sister, decided to elope." Traces of sarcasm suddenly tainted his voice. "Not only did Glenda leave me without child care, but she ran off with my assistant, which leaves me overworked at the office. Nice sister, huh?"

"Nice assistant," Jena quipped.

"Yeah, that too," he muttered.

The man relaxed against the back of the love seat, and Jena noticed his crisp white dress shirt's sleeves were rolled to the elbow. He wore a loosened necktie and black dress pants. Sitting there, Jena thought he looked like he belonged on the cover of *GQ Magazine*.

Her gaze moved back up to the man's face. His gently angled jaw line was clean-shaven, and his lips appeared soft and tender, though bent into a natural smirk. His eyes were a deep brown, and Jena noticed they mirrored her assessment. From his expression, Jena couldn't tell what he thought of her, but in just two words, she figured she could sum him up: handsome and arrogant.

"By the way, my name is Travis Larson."

"Yes, I figured as much."

The smirk broadened. "Well, it's a pleasure to meet you, Miss Calhoun."

She smiled a reply, unsure if she could return the sentiment. "Do you drive?"

"Yes."

"Good. My girls are involved in a lot of activities. Swimming, gymnastics, a weekly playgroup."

"I don't own a car."

Travis waved off her remark. "I do. I own two, in fact. You can use the station wagon."

Jena lifted an inquiring brow. "I can?"

"Maybe this won't be so bad after all," he mused aloud, gazing off into the direction of the sleek, black grand piano, which jutted out from the corner of the living room. His gaze shifted back to Jena. "Do you like children?"

"Yes."

"Are you in school?"

"Yes. I attend Lakeview Bible College."

"Bible college, huh?"

"That's right."

"Are you taking summer classes?"

"No."

"Good."

"Good?" Jena raised surprised brows.

"I wouldn't want your schooling to interfere with your caring for my children."

"Oh. . ."

"What's your major?"

Jena cleared her throat. "Home Economics with a minor in Child Development."

Travis looked taken aback. "Do women still major in those things? Sounds kind of obsolete to me, considering this day and age."

Jena merely shrugged. He was entitled to his opinion, faulty as it was.

"What do you hope to do once you graduate?"

"Manage a daycare center or teach kindergarten in a private school."

"Hmm. . ." He didn't look very impressed. But after a moment's deliberation, a slow grin spread across his face. "You know what? This is perfect! You can practice your home economic skills here in my household and use your child development techniques on my girls. You're hired." Travis stood.

"I am?" Jena stood too. "But—"

"I'll pay you three hundred and fifty dollars a week plus room and board. You'll have access to a car, but I'll take care of all expenses, like gas, tires, tune-ups. In return, I'll expect you to care for my girls from six o'clock A.M. until they go to bed at eight o'clock at night. . .six days a week. You may have Sundays off."

Jena's eyes widened. To her, a poor college student, it sounded like a great deal! She had run out of money last week, after getting laid-off nearly a month ago from her part-time job as a waitress. Fortunately, her wee bit of savings and an unexpected grant had carried her through a few weeks. Then her roommate and best friend, Lisa, moved out of their apartment. Lisa had decided to go back home so she could save money for her upcoming wedding, and now Jena had to be out by the end of the month.

But this job seemed a perfect solution to her financial situation. She'd make a lot more money as Travis Larson's summer girl than she had earned waitressing, and she'd have a car and a place to live until the fall. By then, perhaps, she'd have enough money saved to finish her final semester of college and get another apartment.

"Miss Calhoun?" Travis drawled, sounding like he was preparing to cross-examine a witness. "What do you say? Do Mandi and Carly have a new summer girl?"

Jena looked across the room and straight into Travis Larson's mahogany eyes. Something about his self-assured demeanor troubled her. She wondered if she'd really be able to work for him effectively, a handsome widower with dark, chestnut-colored hair, and an ego the size of Montana. . .

"I want to accept, but—"

"But what?"

"Well, I do need the job; however—"

"However?" He shook his head before arching a perplexed, dark brow. "I don't understand your hesitation."

Jena sighed. Maybe she could work around his ego. She really needed the money. "Could I think about it?"

"Of course." Travis glanced at his wristwatch. "I'll leave the room for, say, ten minutes. How's that?"

Jena gave him a subtle nod. She had really wanted more than ten minutes, but the time allotment would have to do.

True to his word, Travis exited, and Jena sat back down on the sofa. Leaning forward, she folded her hands over her knees and prayed for wisdom. *Lord, what do I do? You know my financial needs. Should I take this job? And what about Mr. Larson? Can I work with him?* She paused in thought. *Can I somehow minister to this family? Is this Your will?*

She mulled over the details. The money sounded great, and she wouldn't mind caring for children all summer. She could be outdoors with them, take them to the beach. "Miss Calhoun?"

Jena lifted her head. "Yes?"

"May I call you Jena?"

"Certainly," she said with a little smile.

"Please call me Travis."

"I'll try," she stated honestly. However, with such a commanding presence, he seemed more like a Mr. Larson.

He left the room again, and Jena continued her inner debate. Maybe he'd turn out to be a really nice guy once she got to know him. She frowned. Were lawyers really "nice guys"?

"Jena?"

She looked up at Travis, standing at the entrance of the living room once more. "Yes?"

"May I show you photographs of my girls?" He stepped forward, holding a picture frame in each hand. "These are this year's school pictures." He handed one to Jena. "That's Amanda Lyn—Mandi, for short."

"Oh, she's cute," Jena said, looking at the little blond girl with the toothless smile and cocoa-colored eyes.

"And this is Carlotta Leann—Carly. She's named after my wife's grandmother."

Jena smiled. "I'll bet she's just as precious as she as looks." Huge brown eyes in a little, round face surrounded by blondish-brown curls peered out from the picture frame. "They're both darling," Jena stated, handing back the photographs.

For the first time, Jena saw Travis's face split into a full-fledged smile. "Thank you." He glanced from one picture to the next. "I'm very proud of my girls and. . .I think the three of you will get along."

Jena still hesitated. After all, her ten minutes weren't up.

Suddenly, his expression fell, and his attitude crumbled along with it. "Look," he said, sitting down beside her, "I'll be honest with you. I'm in a terrible bind. I've got no one to take care of my children and a law firm to run. I've interviewed dozens of summer girl applicants, and I wouldn't leave my goldfish with any of them, let alone my daughters. You are the first decent one to ring my doorbell. And if Mrs. Barlow says you're 'a sweet girl,' I trust it's true. Mrs. Barlow has been my next door neighbor for the last eight years, and she's one tough old lady—no offense intended," he added quickly. "I mean quite the opposite, really."

Jena was stunned by his candidness.

So stunned, she accepted the job.

"Oh, that's great," Travis said, smiling, and Jena thought he actually looked. . .grateful! Then he glanced at the framed photographs, still in his hands, before looking back at her. "Just one more thing, Jena."

"What's that?"

He paused and his gaze returned to hers. His dark eyes held an almost pleading look. "Can you start today?"

two

"Okay, you can come down now," Travis called up the stairs.

A couple of doors squeaked open, and two pairs of feet came running down the carpeted steps.

"Was she another dud, Daddy?"

Jena looked expectantly at Travis, but he didn't even glance her way. He just smiled fondly at the little girl hugging him around the knees.

"Hardly a dud, Sweetie. We've got ourselves a summer girl. Look." The little girls peered curiously at Jena, and Travis made the introductions.

"She doesn't look like a summer girl, Daddy," Mandi said precociously.

"Well, maybe we'll call her your new nanny, then."

"You know, I really would rather be a summer girl," Jena interjected. She smiled at Travis's surprised expression and added, "Summer is my favorite time of year."

"Mine too!" exclaimed Mandi.

"Mine too!" little Carly mimicked.

"Terrific!" Travis said with a clap of hands. "I can tell you two girls are going to like Jena."

"Miss Jena," she corrected. At Travis's wondering glance, she explained, "During my internship last year, I learned that it's best for children to address adults respectfully by using a preface such as Miss, Mister, or Missus. But your girls don't have to use my last name, since I think that would be too formal for this situation. They may simply refer to me as Miss Jena."

"I see." The smirk returned, and Travis looked much like

that handsome, arrogant man Jena saw just minutes ago. "Any other rules that I should be aware of. . .Miss Jena?"

"Hmm. . .well, no, I think that's it," she replied, feeling her face warm with embarrassment.

"Good." Travis turned to his daughters. "Mandi, Carly, Miss Jena is going to be your new summer girl." He suddenly frowned and looked back at Jena. "Somehow that doesn't sound quite right, the words 'Miss Jena' and 'summer girl' in the same sentence."

"I know, Daddy," Mandi said, "Miss Jena can be our summer lady."

Travis laughed. "All right. Summer lady it is."

Jena shrugged, feeling more than a little chagrined now.

"Can the girls and I show you the apartment you'll be staying in?"

"Sure." She followed Travis and his daughters who bounced and skipped beside their daddy. They walked through the kitchen, out the back door, and into the courtyard which was more like an enclosed patio complete with a round, white wrought-iron table, and matching chairs. They passed under the walkway until they arrived at another door. It was painted white and a little half-moon seemed to be smiling lopsidedly at her.

Travis pulled a ring of keys from out of his pocket and unlocked the door. "The apartment is pretty much furnished," he told Jena. "My sister used to live up here."

"But then she married Tony," Mandi stated informatively. "And now Daddy has no one to watch me and Carly."

"Yes, I do," Travis replied as they all walked up the polished, wooden stairs. "I have Miss Jena to watch you."

"Oh, yeah."

Chuckling at his daughter, Travis unlocked another door at the top of the stairs. They all entered the living room where the two girls made for the overstuffed sofa and flounced on it as though they'd done it a thousand times before. They sank into it, all giggles and flailing limbs.

Smiling, Jena looked around the room. The walls were a dusty-rose, the woodwork painted white. Ivory draperies hung on four large windows that looked out over the quiet, tree-lined avenue. A deep maroon fabric covered the sofa, the same color as the carpet. In the corner stood a small tea table and chair, and on the adjacent wall were two built-in bookshelves.

"After my wife, Meg, died," Travis explained, "I supplied this apartment with our old furniture so my sister would be comfortable up here. Then I bought new items for my place, thinking they would somehow ease the pain of losing my wife."

"Did they?" Jena inquired softly.

Travis gave her a pointed stare. "Nope. Not a bit." He quickly changed the subject. "Mandi, Carly. . .let's show Miss Jena the rest of her new home, shall we?"

"Okay, but I'll do it, Daddy," Mandi said. She jumped off the sofa and took Jena's hand. "This is where you eat," the little girl said as they entered the dining room.

Jena surveyed the soft-pink walls, the same color of the living room. A white dining set and four matching chairs occupied the center of the dining area. Against one wall was a built-in china hutch, and Jena decided that this was nicer than any dining room in any apartment she had lived in since she'd left home.

Then suddenly, she thought of her family. Jena wished she could phone them and share the news of this blessing—and, yes, she already sensed this job was a Godsend. Unfortunately, her family probably couldn't care less. They'd never been close, and only Jena claimed Christ as her Savior; the rest of her family members resided in determined unbelief.

Still, she prayed for them daily and trusted the Lord to

change their hearts as only He could. Jena also prayed that she'd have a close-knit family someday—a family that loved each other and enjoyed doing things together, unlike her own parents and brother who had always operated independently of each other. In fact, her family background was why Jena had selected home economics and child development as her fields of study—she longed for a real family someday, and she was determined to do the best job possible in caring for it.

"And this is where you cook," Mandi told her, pulling her into the kitchen.

The room was tiny, but the whitewashed walls and matching mini-blinds made it seem like less of a cracker box. An apartment-sized refrigerator and stove, a standard-sized sink, and a very narrow counter were the kitchen's only fixtures. Nevertheless, it appeared practical enough.

"This is your bedroom," Mandi said, running forward, then sailing headlong onto the bed. Carly followed right behind her, and soon both little girls were jumping on the bare mattress.

"All right, that's enough," Travis told them, lifting each child off the bed. "I have no time to take you to the hospital for stitches today." He looked at Jena. "My sister had her own bedding and towels which she took with her, so I'll have to purchase some for you."

"That's not necessary. I own those essentials."

Travis shrugged his broad shoulders. "Well, okay. But if you need anything else, let me know."

"I will. Thanks."

"Here's the bathroom, Miss Jena!" Mandi cried excitedly. Her dark eyes sparkled, and when she smiled, the entire hallway seemed to light up.

"I see your front teeth have come in since you had your school picture taken," Jena remarked, and Mandi smiled even broader to show off her two new pearly whites.

Jena peered around the pixie and looked into the bathroom. It was more than adequate, and she whispered a prayer of thanks for such a comfortable place in which she could live.

"You can do your laundry in my washer and dryer," Travis offered. "Just do it during the day, because I usually wash our clothes at night. My sister would usually throw in a load while the girls were watching TV and while dinner was cooking."

"So I'm to make supper?"

Travis nodded, but then his expression turned to one of concern. "You can cook, can't you?"

"Oh, yes," Jena replied, smiling. "In fact, I love to cook!"

"Well, that'll be a nice change," Travis said on a facetious note. "Glenda's specialty was macaroni and cheese out of the box."

"And peanut butter and jelly," Carly piped up happily.

Travis smiled at his youngest, then back at Jena. "I don't often make it home for dinner, though," he informed her, "so you don't have to worry about me. Just feed the girls. . .and yourself, of course."

"Sometimes Aunty Glenda let us eat up here with her," Mandi said.

Carly nodded. "We had a picklenic."

"A picnic," Mandi corrected.

Little Carly just nodded.

"How fun," Jena said warmly, although she felt a little sorry for Travis. He doesn't often make it home for dinner with his daughters, she mused. And, sadly, it reminded her of her own upbringing, her parents working constantly with little or no time to spend with their children. Jena and her brother often fended for themselves in between the wide gamut of sitters that came and went.

"Well?" Travis asked, bringing Jena out of her thoughts.

"What do you think?"

"I think I'll be very comfortable here," she replied gratefully. "Thank you."

"You're welcome. When can you move in?"

Jena chewed her lower lip in contemplation. She had to be out of her apartment by the end of the month, which was just days away, and she didn't have much to pack. "I don't know," she said at last. "Any time, I guess."

"Great." Travis pulled three keys off his ring. "This is for the car," he said, putting in into Jena's palm, "this is your apartment key, and this is for my house."

Jena looked them over and nodded.

"Move in whenever you like. Today would be fine with me, and I'm sure the girls would love to help you move."

Mandi and Carly both nodded exuberantly.

"But my apartment. . .it's in Jefferson County," Jena said. "Or don't you mind me taking the girls that distance?"

"Are you a good driver?"

"Well, yes, I suppose I am."

"Speeding tickets?"

"Never!" she exclaimed.

An amused expression crossed Travis's face. "Okay, just make sure the girls wear their seatbelts. You can use the station wagon to haul all your stuff over here."

"Well, the good news is I'll only have to make one trip," Jena informed her new employer. "I don't have a whole lot." She snapped her fingers. "Oh, but I forgot. . .I'll have to return my apartment key at my landlord's house if I move out today."

"Where does your landlord live?"

"Just a few miles from the college I attend, but it'll take extra time. Next, I'll have to put in a change of address at the post office. . ."

"Jena, do whatever you have to do, just take Mandi and

Carly with you. Have them help you. It'll be good for them, and it'll be great for me," he added emphatically.

"Okay, sure."

They all walked back through the apartment and out the front door. Travis waited for Jena to lock it before continuing down the stairs.

"Anything else I should know?" she asked.

Travis thought it over, then shook his head. "I don't think so. But here," he said, pulling out his wallet, "let me give you my business card so you can phone me if something urgent arises. I have an extra cell phone you can use." He handed her the card, followed by a fifty-dollar bill.

Jena gave him a quizzical frown. "What's this for?"

"Dinner. . .and whatever else you might need to pick up. There's not a lot of food in the house." He turned pensive before pressing another twenty-dollar bill into her palm. "Come to think of it, we really don't have any food in the house."

Jena tried not to laugh. "Don't worry. The girls and I will go grocery shopping right after we get my things and finish my errands." She turned to the little faces gazing up at her. "Mandi and Carly," she said with a smile, "we have our work cut out for us today!"

three

Jena dialed the cell phone number of her friend, Mary Star Palmer, to say she didn't need a ride back to school. When Star heard Jena got the job, she was almost as relieved as Jena.

"Now we just have to find me a summer job," Star said. "I'm not getting any bites here at the mall."

"Well, let's keep praying about it. . .and I'll call you later."

After hanging up the Larsons' phone, which hung on the kitchen wall, Jena scooted the girls into the car. Taking a few minutes to familiarize herself with the dashboard, she stuck the key into the ignition and backed out of the garage. As she neared her apartment, Jena stopped at a local fast-food restaurant and ordered lunch. A deep fried aroma of cheeseburgers and French fries filled Travis Larson's Volvo wagon, and Jena promised herself she would eat healthier at dinnertime. After they arrived at the dingy shoebox of a place that Jena called home, she seated Mandi and Carly at the scuffed-up table, then served lunch.

"Wait, don't eat yet," Jena said just as Mandi bit into her burger. "We have to pray."

The girls glanced at each other, then looked, wide-eyed, at Jena, who folded her hands and bowed her head. Peeking over her lashes, she watched as Mandi and Carly followed her lead.

"Thank You, Jesus, for this food. Please use it to make our bodies strong so we can get all our work done this afternoon. In Your name, we pray. . .Amen." Lifting her gaze, she smiled at the girls. "Okay, now we can eat."

They regarded her with curiosity shining in their brown eyes.

"Do you pray at your house?" Jena asked.

With mouths full, they both shook their heads.

"Do you know who Jesus is?"

Mandi and Carly bobbed their heads and smiled.

"He's God," Mandi said after swallowing her food. "Mrs. Barlow told us about Him."

"Wonderful!"

"And God made this whole world," Carly declared, spreading her arms with a dramatic flare that caused Jena to grin. "He even made this hamburger!"

"No, people at the restaurant made the hamburgers," Mandi retorted.

"You're both right," Jena cut in before a heated debate ensued. "God made the cows, and cows are the beef, and the beef is what the cooks at the restaurant use to make the hamburgers."

"See," Mandi told her little sister.

The reply was all but lost on Carly who started a new subject about cows that lasted for the remainder of lunchtime. Once they'd finished eating, Jena instructed the girls as to how to clean up.

"My mom died," Mandi blurted, as she tossed her hamburger wrapper in the trash.

"Yes, I know," Jena said on a rueful note. "Your dad mentioned it. How did she die?"

"She had cancer."

"I'm sorry to hear that." Jena's heart went out to the little girl.

Carly, on the other hand, seemed oblivious to the conversation as she balanced on her tiptoes and deposited her garbage into the blue, tall plastic bin.

Mandi didn't say anymore about her mother, so Jena didn't push the subject. Instead, she assigned tasks. She pulled out the small canister vacuum cleaner and showed Mandi how to use it. Next, she gave Carly a spray bottle of the organic orange non-poisonous "cleans everything" solution her friend Lisa used to sell and showed the little girl how to wipe down the furniture.

"Do a good job for me so I'll get my security deposit back, all right?"

"What's a s'curity posit?" Carly asked as she sprayed the liquid onto a table.

"That's the money I had to put down on this apartment when I first moved in. If I leave this place nice and clean, my landlord will give me my money back."

"Down worry," Mandi said, "we're good cleaners. You'll get your money back."

Jena smiled, and with Mandi and Carly now occupied, she began opening drawers and closets, stuffing things into boxes. Since the apartment came furnished, there wasn't much to pack. Before long, the air smelled like a ripe orange grove. Mandi had finished vacuuming and decided to dust with Carly. The two left no surface untouched.

A while later, Jena had the Volvo packed with everything she owned. *My life in the back of a station wagon,* she thought, feeling a bit blue. But then she heard the girls' giggling as they jumped off the apartment building's front steps, and she realized that things weren't all that important in life. What mattered most were people.

"Mandi. Carly," she called, opening the door to the back-seat. "Let's go. We've got to drop off my keys and stop at the grocery store."

Carly pouted. "But that's going to take twenty weeks!" she said, waving her hands in a theatrical manner.

Jena laughed. "It better not."

"How come?" Mandi wanted to know as she climbed into the deep-green colored car.

"Because in twenty weeks, I'll be back in school. My last

semester, then I graduate. . .YES!"

"How come you can't stay with us forever?" Carly asked as Jena fastened the seatbelt around her.

"Well, because—" Jena felt her heart constrict. *These poor kids! First, their mother dies, then their aunt takes off and gets married, and now I'm counting the days until I'm back in school.* "I can't stay with you forever," she tried again, "because I'm not part of your family. But we can always be friends, okay?"

"Okay," Carly agreed with an easy smile.

"My Aunty Glenda is part of our family," Mandi countered with a perception far beyond her six years, "but she can't stay with us forever because she married Tony."

Jena didn't know what to say. Relationships in her own family unit had been cast off, discarded. Did anything last forever in this throwaway society?

"Know what? The truth is, only Jesus lasts forever. He'll stay by you and never leave you for anything. Now that's a happy thought, isn't it?"

The girls nodded, and Mandi turned to gaze out the window. Carly kicked her sandaled feet up and down.

"Can we go now, Miss Jena?" Carly said. "Twenty weeks is gonna come really fast."

"Yes, it is," Jena agreed with a little laugh. "And you're right. We can't sit around chatting all day. There's lots of work to be done before twenty weeks are up!"

&

"I'm glad you got your babysitting problems taken care of, Trav."

He nodded in reply to Craig Duncan's comment. As the senior partner of Duncan, Duncan, and Larson, Craig had shouldered the burdens caused by Travis's many absences since Glenda left.

"Do you think you'll be prepared to take the Hamland case tomorrow?"

"Oh, sure. Not a problem. I'm very familiar with the case."

"Good."

Craig sat back in his burgundy leather office chair and put his feet up on his paper-laden desk. "So what's this girl like?"

"What girl?" Travis asked, preoccupied with the file he held.

"The one you hired to baby-sit!"

"Oh. . .sorry, Craig." Travis looked up and gave the grizzled older man his undivided attention. "She's great. Her name is Jena. She's in her mid-twenties, just finishing up college, and she needs a job for the summer."

"Interesting. . ."

"And she's a home ec major." Travis gazed back at the contents in the file.

"Oh, is she?" Craig rubbed his grizzled jaw. "Well, this does sound like a perfect match, doesn't it? Too bad she can't earn a couple of college credits while she works for you."

Travis shrugged. "That's her department."

Craig chuckled. "You're all heart, Trav."

The quip caused him to grin, and he glanced back at his business partner. Since the day they met, Craig reminded him of a mad scientist. Gray, fluffy hair, keen blue eyes. An intelligent man, but somewhat scatterbrained. Capable, but highly disorganized. Craig's son, Josh, on the other hand, was the extreme opposite. Stout and blond, Josh threw conniption fits if paperclips in his desk drawer weren't in their proper place. Most of the time, Travis felt his duty in the office was to serve as some sort of balance between the two men and to encourage Marci, their secretary who threatened to quit every other Friday.

Then there was Yolanda. The dark-haired beauty was the firm's intern, and if there ever existed a woman whom Travis would hate to come up against in court, it would be her. She could dig up dirt on Mother Teresa.

"So, is she pretty?" Craig asked.

"Who?"

"Your summer girl!"

Travis gave himself a mental shake. "Oh, yeah, she's okay." He thought about Jena's full figure—a little too full for his liking. But she had pretty hair, shoulder-length strawberry-blond. She had an oval, freckled face with a healthy complexion. But her blue eyes said more than her naturally pink lips, and as she sized him up this morning, Travis could tell he didn't measure up to her standards. He saw it in her expression, as cut and dry as the Hamland's lawsuit. Of course, he really didn't care what Jena Calhoun thought of him personally. He'd hired her to take care of his daughters, not him.

"Okay? Just okay?" Craig chuckled and lifted his feet off the desk. "Well, she must have impressed you if you left your most precious commodities with her, having only made her acquaintance this morning."

"Sure, she impressed me. She's got that wholesome motherly look about her, and she goes to a Bible college, which means she's probably honest and trustworthy, and my neighbor Mrs. Barlow gave her a glowing recommendation. That pretty much cinched it for me."

Craig pursed his thick lips and sniffed. "Look, Trav, I hope it works out for you. You're a partner in this law firm, and we need you here."

"I understand, and things are going to work out great," he replied, perceiving the comments as something of a threat. If he didn't pull his weight, Craig and Josh could easily let someone buy him out. Yolanda might be a candidate. She had the ability to sway Craig with amazing ease, and he frequently took her side on the various issues which had emerged in recent weeks. Moreover, Craig owned the deciding shares.

That's why he needed Jena, and Travis felt a twinge of desperation at the thought of her quitting her position. He had muddled through the last month while Mandi was in school and Carly in daycare. But now that summer was here, he would much prefer the girls be at home, enjoying the sunshine and less hectic schedule. If they caught a cold, Jena could nurse them back to health, and he wouldn't have to ask a colleague to cover him in court as he'd done in the past. On the nights he worked until midnight—or beyond—Jena could have the girls fed and tucked into bed by the time he came home so he could pick up where he'd left off at the office.

Yes, Jena had to work out. And if there truly was a God in heaven like Meg used to insist, then He would see to it that these arrangements were a success. Mandi and Carly's well-being depended on it.

And so did his career.

four

When Travis walked into the back hall at seven fifty-five, the enticing smell of oregano and garlic met him. He made his way into the kitchen and placed his briefcase on the table, along with the bag of greasy tacos he'd purchased on the way home. The glass pan on the stove caught his eye. He crossed the brightly decorated room and peeled back the tin foil.

"Lasagna." Travis's mouth began to water, and his stomach rumbled.

Suddenly, he heard a loud boom above him, and he suspected his oldest daughter had just jumped off her bed—something he was forever telling her not to do. She'd crack the plaster ceiling one of these days—either that or crack her skull.

He listened as thundering footfalls raced across the second floor and down the steps.

"Daddy's home!" the girls cried in succession. "Hi, Daddy!"

He knelt down to receive their welcome. His exuberant daughters nearly knocked him onto his back. "Hey, little princesses. . ." They smelled good, like baby shampoo and pretty pink lotion. He kissed them and gave them each a squeeze. "What are you still doing awake?"

"Miss Jena said we could come down for a goodnight kiss," Mandi informed him.

"Ah. . ."

"But now we hafta go back up to hear the rest of our story," Carly chimed in.

"*Winnie the Pooh,*" Mandi announced, "but it's not the baby picture book. It's the real book."

Travis lifted his brows, hoping he looked impressed.

"But Miss Jena is letting Carly look at the picture book while she reads to us."

"I see." Travis stood. "Well don't let me keep you."

He grinned as his girls took off running, then Mandi did a one-eighty.

"I forgot to tell you. . .we made lasagna."

"I see that. Looks great!"

"And there's salad in the fridge that we made, but it has chunks of stuff in it." The six year old wrinkled her nose. "I didn't like it. But Miss Jena says we should try new things."

"Chunks of stuff?" Travis almost laughed aloud at the description. "What kind of stuff?"

"I don't remember what it's called," she said, padding to the refrigerator, swinging the door open, and pulling out the wooden salad bowl. She picked a 'chunk' out of the green leafy contents and handed it to him. "That's it. Yuck."

"That's an artichoke heart," Travis said, popping it into his mouth. "Yum."

"Glad you like it, 'cause I sure don't," Mandi said, handing him the bowl and trotting out of the kitchen. "Night, night."

"Good night." Travis smiled as he picked out another 'chunk of stuff' and ate it.

This is great, he thought, *lasagna, salad. . .* He set the bowl on the table and, on a hunch, peeked into the oven. There it was, wrapped in foil. . .and garlic bread. All right!

Plate in hand, Travis carved a wide slab out of the pan. He put the lasagna in the microwave for a minute, then added the salad, lightly seasoned with oil and vinegar, and the garlic bread. Carrying his dinner into his study, he decided he could get used to this, coming home to find supper all ready for him. But he wouldn't. He figured Jena had just set out to impress him on her first day, and—after one bite—he was impressed. After all, Glenda never cooked.

His sister's elopement still angered him. Glenda knew he needed her. She had promised to stick by him, help him out—but, of course, it had cost him plenty. Jena's salary paled next to his sister's.

Travis tried to focus on the newspaper as he ate, but he kept thinking of Glenda, which rekindled his aggravation. He loved his sister, but her leaving had put him in an awful bind, and life in general had been so incredibly difficult since Meg died. Many a night Travis had cried himself to sleep, knowing he'd never again hold his beloved wife in his arms. But it wasn't as if he didn't have time to prepare for her passing. Just after discovering she was expecting Carly, Meg learned she had ovarian cancer. The doctor urged her to give up her baby, but Meg refused, and the cancer spread quickly. By the time Carly was just about full term, Meg had barely the strength to deliver her. But she sure had the determination, and a healthy baby girl arrived in the world. Travis had never resented Carly, and he was always surprised when friends mustered the courage to ask that question. No, Carly was a special gift from the woman he loved with all his being. In fact, he was hard-pressed at times not to show partiality toward Carly. Mandi was a special little girl too.

Setting down his fork, Travis stared at his half-eaten meal. He'd been so hungry when he delved in, but he'd suddenly lost his appetite.

"Excuse me. . ."

Travis jumped at the feminine voice—one he was very unaccustomed to hearing. He looked toward the doorway and found Jena standing there, dressed in the same outfit she'd worn this morning, a loose-fitting, navy blue shirt and a gypsy-looking skirt. On her feet were strappy brown sandals.

"Sorry," she said, "I didn't mean to sneak up on you."

"No, problem," he fibbed. "What's up?"

"Well, the girls are just about asleep, and since it's after eight, I thought I'd go next door and start unpacking."

"Sure. Go ahead. . .and you did a great job today. Thanks." He nodded at his plate. "Food's delicious."

"Good."

She smiled, and Travis noticed the two bright pink spots that suddenly appeared on her cheeks. It amazed him a little. He didn't know many women who blushed these days.

"Um. . .if you don't mind me saying so, you look really tired. Can I get you anything before I leave?"

"Naw," he sat back in his desk chair and crossed his foot to his knee. "I'm fine."

She looked disappointed, and her expression piqued his curiosity. He furrowed his brows.

"Okay, I'll confess," she said, obviously noting his frown. "I had an ulterior motive for asking that last question. You see, I have a ton of things to get done, and I'm a coffee freak, so I was hoping you'd say you wanted some coffee, then I'd have a great excuse to make a pot and help myself to a very large mug of it before I left."

Travis chuckled. "Why didn't you just say so?"

She shrugged. "I was trying to be polite."

"I see. . .well, sure. . .I'll have a cup. I'm planning to burn the midnight oil myself. But do we have coffee?"

"Ohhhh, yeah," she drawled. "We have coffee. That went into the shopping cart before the milk and eggs."

He laughed again. "Go for it. Brew to your heart's content."

"Great. Thanks."

She spun around, her skirt flaring, and headed for the kitchen. Travis pushed his plate aside and tossed the newspaper onto the floor. Then he opened his attaché case and withdrew the Hamland file. After some time of reading through the case, the rich aromatic smell of some sort of flavored coffee teased his nostrils and distracted him enough that he decided to take his plate into the kitchen and pour a cup. When he entered the kitchen, he found it empty, save for the gurgling coffee maker. Through the space between the lacy valance and yellow and white café curtains, he saw through the window that Glenda's light was on.

But it's not Glenda's place anymore. It's Jena's. . .at least for the summer. Travis tried not to think about what he would do come fall. One day at a time.

Exhaling a long, weary sigh, he figured he might as well throw in a load of wash before he buckled down to work. He made his way to the basement, noticing the girls' toys were picked up in the playroom. For the first time in a very long time, he could actually see the red, yellow, and green geometrically designed carpet and—he took a sniff—it smelled oddly of oranges.

Sure hope the kids didn't spill something down here.

He walked into the laundry area and stopped dead in his tracks. There on top of the shining white washer was a basket of folded clothes.

She did the laundry too?

Travis couldn't believe it. Dinner, clean playroom, clean children. . .and clean clothes.

But, of course, it was too good to be true.

Okay, she earned her money today. Travis walked up the stairwell. *But let's just see how long this lasts.*

He thought of his sister, Miss Lazybones herself. She barely dragged herself out of bed before he left for work. Most times, Travis had to send the girls over to wake their aunty up. Her idea of "making supper" was ordering Chinese food, pizza, or buying frozen dinners that she could just heat up. Just as he'd informed Jena, macaroni and cheese out of the box was Glenda's specialty. Rarely were the girls ready for bed when he got home, and often they were dirty from playing outside or at a neighbor's house. Glenda watched every daytime drama on TV, and those shows were often the topic of heated debates, since Travis didn't want his young daughters exposed to the adult themes and steamy love scenes. Her nighttime television habits weren't much better.

But at least she'd been a responsible person, for the most part. She practically raised Carly. She sang to them and played games with them. For all her faults, the girls loved her.

So did Travis. Glenda was his baby sister, after all—except he still felt a strong urge to take her over his knee for abandoning him without notice. However, he quickly reminded himself that his worries were over. He had hired a summer girl now. He had hired Jena.

❧

The sun crept up the eastern sky amid splashes of pink, maroon, and gray, and the wind felt warm against her skin as Jena traipsed across the teeny courtyard to the main house. She stuck the key into the lock and let herself in. Day Two on the job was about to begin, and the weather promised to be beautiful.

As she made a pot of strong coffee in the charming kitchen, papered in blue and white checks with tiny pink flowers at each corner, Jena began thinking over the things she wanted to accomplish. Of course, she would have to confer with Mr. Larson before she set her plans in motion. He mentioned the girls had scheduled activities. . .did he say swimming lessons?

Extracting a slip of paper from the back pocket of her denim skirt, Jena scanned the recipe for her favorite scrambled egg casserole. She had hurried to copy it by hand out of a fat recipe book before leaving her apartment. Within minutes, she had all the necessary ingredients on the counter. Eggs, milk, green pepper, a package of precooked sausage, which she'd put in the fridge overnight to thaw, and cheddar cheese. She sliced and mixed, then turned it all over into a casserole dish and slid it into the oven.

Jena stood back, feeling elated. A family to cook for and dote upon. . .what a dream come true. Best of all, she'd get paid for it.

As a girl growing up in a bustling suburb of Los Angeles, she usually did all the cooking and cleaning at home. Her mother worked a full-time job, and her father was a fireman who wasn't home much. Consequently, Jena mothered her mother, took care of her father, and practically raised her brother. . .and those were the good days. The bad days began while Jena was in high school. Her mother had her career, her father had his, and Geoffrey, her "baby brother," was enrolled in every sports program and co-curricular activity the school offered. They had their own lives, apart from each other, and worse, apart from God. There were no in-depth conversations taking place in the home. No one cared how the other fared, as long as somebody didn't interfere with schedules and appointments.

Watching her family grow further and further apart broke Jena's heart. She tried to round them up for dinner, but it didn't work. She tried to corner them individually so she could tell them about her faith in Christ, but they were too busy to listen. When she chose to attend Lakeview Bible College in Wisconsin, her father said he wouldn't pay for it—he wouldn't even help her out. He thought she should join the military and get her education paid for through the government. But Jena prayed about it and felt the Army wasn't God's will for her life. Her mother thought she should go into interior design and attend the junior college in L.A. But, again, Jena knew God wanted her in Wisconsin. So she saved her money and stepped out in faith. She hadn't seen her family in nearly four years. She phoned them every once in a while, but there wasn't much to say. She wrote letters and sent E-mails, but replies were few and far between. Her mother, father, and brother were her blood relatives; she had lived with them for most of her life, but Jena didn't know them at all.

The drumming of little feet running upstairs brought her out of her reverie. Next, a Scripture verse flittered across her mind. *No one who puts his hand to the plow and looks back is fit for service in the kingdom of God.*

Jena shook herself. *Dear Lord, forgive me for dwelling in the past. You brought me halfway across the country to grow me up in Your word, and You've got a job for me to do.*

At that precise moment, Mandi and Carly skipped into the kitchen.

five

"What's all this?" Travis asked, entering the kitchen. Dressed in a starched and pressed light blue dress shirt and dark pants, he held his attaché case in one hand, while he juggled his matching suit jacket and a coordinating tie in the other.

Jena gave him a polite smile and set Carly's plate of eggs in front of her. "This is breakfast." She caught a whiff of the sweet-woodsy scent of Travis's cologne and thought it smelled quite appealing.

"So I see. . .but we usually don't do breakfast. I mean, the girls might have cereal or something. . ."

"Breakfast is the most important meal of the day," Jena said, scooping out some of her scrambled egg casserole for him. Next, she placed it on the round table and held her hand out, indicating he should sit down in between the girls.

Travis gnawed the corner of his lip, appearing contemplative.

"It's really good, Daddy," Mandi said.

"I'm sure it is."

"And look how we set the table!" Carly exclaimed.

"I noticed." He glanced at his wristwatch. "Well, okay, I've got a few minutes."

Travis deposited his briefcase, jacket, and tie on the long counter. Taking his seat at the table, he lifted his fork and began to eat.

"Daddy, you forgot to pray," Mandi chided him.

Jena couldn't help a grimace as she stood with her back to the table pouring Travis a cup of coffee. She hoped he wouldn't mind that she taught the girls to ask God's blessing on their food at every meal.

"Your prayer counted for me too," Travis replied with a mouthful.

Jena rolled her eyes. *Okay, Lord, I guess I have a way to go here. . .*

She set the steaming mug in front of him. "Cream or sugar or both, Mr. Larson?"

He peered up at her with a puzzled expression. "Just sugar. . .and I thought we were on a first name basis. . .Jena."

"It's Miss Jena, Daddy," Mandi corrected him.

Carly nodded, her little cheeks bulging with food.

When he glanced back at her, Jena had to laugh at the bested look on his face. "I'll get the sugar bowl for you. . . Travis."

"Hey, that's Mister Travis," Mandi scolded.

"Stop being so bossy and eat your breakfast," he told her.

"That's Miss Bossy," Carly said.

Travis chuckled, and Jena even had to laugh as she placed the sugar on the table. But then she noticed Mandi's indignant expression and quickly walked over to the little girl. Standing behind her, Jena gently massaged her upper arms.

"It was just a little joke. Don't be upset. We know you're not really Miss Bossy." She kissed the top of Mandi's blond head. "You just like things done right—and that's good."

She nodded, and peering around her, Jena saw that her scrunched up features had softened.

Travis gave his oldest a charming wink, and Mandi returned a shy smile.

Jena straightened and rubbed her palms together. "So what's on the agenda for today, Mr. Travis? Do the girls have any lessons or play groups that I need to get them to at a certain hour?"

He wiped his mouth with a paper napkin. "Today's Tuesday,

so that means Mandi has swimming lessons this morning at ten o'clock. After that, the day's yours."

"Okay. We'll think of something fun to do this afternoon."

"Great, and I'll get a schedule together for you. I'll give it to you tonight."

"That would be most helpful," Jena replied, thinking Travis Larson didn't appear to be half as egotistical as she'd first thought yesterday.

After a few more bites and a swig of coffee, he wiped his mouth and stood. "I've got to get going." He gave each of his daughters a loving smooch before adding the old fatherly warning of "Be good."

Then, he strode over to Jena who moved aside so he could reclaim his tie and briefcase.

"I wasn't sure if you needed it or not, but I packed you a lunch." The fat brown bag sat on the counter near his tie, and she slid it toward him.

He stared at it, wearing a curious look. "I don't usually take a lunch, but. . .what is it?"

"Oh, nothing really, just a piece of leftover lasagna and a small salad. I didn't put dressing on it, so the lettuce wouldn't get soggy."

Travis scooped up the bag. "Thanks."

Jena followed him through the kitchen to the back hall in case there were any last minute instructions.

"Um. . .thanks for doing the laundry. You didn't have to."

"Yes, I did. I needed to wash some clothes and your stuff was in both the washer and dryer."

Travis pivoted, and she saw him wince. "Sorry 'bout that. I wasn't expecting you, so—"

"It's okay. Not a problem."

He replied with a hint of a smile and opened the door.

"Have a good day," she said.

"Yeah, you too."

With that, he exited the house, and Jena walked back into the kitchen. Mandi and Carly both watched her with expectant grins, causing her to feel like doing something silly. Lifting her arms, she let out a whoop, before shouting, "We're going to have a fun day today!"

The girls caught the excitement. They laughed and jumped off their chairs.

"C'mon, Carly, let's go get dressed."

Jena chuckled as the girls ran out of the room, imitating the hoot she'd just produced. Glancing around at the glasses, plates, and crusty casserole dish, she figured she had about ten minutes—if that—in which to clean up the kitchen.

☙

Life seemed good again as Travis drove back to his office. After six hours in court, the judge had ruled in his favor in the Hamland case. Travis felt like he was back on top of the world.

Parking his sleek, black Lexus, he sauntered into the busy downtown office building and rode the elevator to the tenth floor. Stepping out of the car, he walked down the muted yellow marble thoroughfare to the glass doors on which the names DUNCAN, DUNCAN, & LARSON were etched in gold lettering.

"We–ell, congratulations," Craig greeted him in the lobby of their office suites. "Nice day in court."

"Oh, honestly," Yolanda Timmerman muttered from behind the receptionist's desk, "an idiot could have won that case. It was obvious the company was negligent in Mr. Hamland's injury."

Travis bit back a retort. He'd worked hard, done his research, and he'd won fair and square. . .and he wasn't an idiot, either!

"Trav, I need to talk to you," Craig said. "Follow me into my office."

"Sure."

He didn't bother to look in Yolanda's direction. He didn't need to see her exotic, dark features to know that her lips were curved in a mocking smile.

Entering Craig's office, Travis shut the door behind him. "Isn't her internship up yet?"

Craig chuckled. "Sit down, Travis."

Setting his briefcase on the adjacent armchair, he did as Craig bid him. "What's up?"

"Oh, nothing really. . .just a minor inconvenience."

Travis began to worry. "What kind of inconvenience?"

"Isabella Minniati."

Travis winced at the name of the top executive of a local sports team—one that D D & L was courting and hoped to represent. "What hoops does Bella want us to jump through this time?"

"Oh. . . ," Craig waved a nonchalant hand in the air, ". . .she's suddenly big on families, kids, and pets." He lifted a busy brow. "She's expecting, you know?"

Travis lifted a brow of his own. "Is she? Well, congratulate her for me."

Craig grinned. "You can congratulate her yourself. I've invited her to dinner on Thursday night to celebrate her newest, um, discovery."

"Obviously you want me to be there."

"Well, of course. . .seeing as dinner will be at your house."

"What?! My house?" He shook his head. "No. Won't work."

"Travis, it's a perfect backdrop. You have a comfortable home. Your daughters are as cute as koalas, and your home ec summer girl can whip something up for dinner."

"I can't ask Jena to do that."

"The firm will pay her. Tell her we'll give her. . .oh, a hundred bucks."

"A caterer would cost two grand."

"Yes, well, all the more reason to have your summer girl put her skills to good use."

"What if she bombs? What if dinner is a complete disaster?" Travis didn't really believe it would happen, but there was always that possibility.

"The answer's simple. We'll explain to Bella that your summer girl is but a mere college student, and we'll laugh it off. Then we'll order a pizza."

"Let's just order pizza to begin with."

"Now, Travis, we owe it to your summer girl to prepare her for life. What if she winds up marrying some businessman whose job requires him to entertain? You don't want that poor girl to be completely in the dark, do you? We're offering her a chance to gain valuable experience."

Travis laughed. "That's quite a stretch, Craig. How long did it take you to think up that logic?"

"About as long as it took you to convince Judge Thompson that Dwight Hamland is now permanently disabled because he bent over to pick up a quarter that accidentally flew out of the vending machine he was working on at the shop."

"There was a little more to it than that." Travis stood and lifted his briefcase. "But I'll talk to Jena and let you know what she says. I'll warn you, though, I'm not going to coerce her into doing anything that she's not comfortable with. The last thing I need is for her to quit on me."

"True, true. . ." Craig leaned back in his chair. "But give it your best shot. You're a persuasive guy, and there's millions of dollars riding on this deal."

Then why be so cheap? Travis wondered, leaving Craig's office for his own. Then, again, that was Craig Duncan's middle name—Cheap. He sighed and entered his office. Maybe he'd just go ahead and hire a caterer and leave Jena out of this.

❧

"Are you sure your new boss won't care that I'm here visiting you while you're on the job?" Mary Star Palmer asked.

Kneeling on the pavement in the tiny courtyard as she and the girls planted flowers, Jena glanced over her shoulder. "No, I don't think he'll care. It's not like I'm neglecting my duties."

"Do you want some help?"

Jena smiled at her blond, blue-eyed friend. "No. We're just about finished. You just relax and drink your lemonade. You've had a rough day."

"Amen! I'm telling you. . .there's not a job to be had in this entire city." Star sighed.

"Maybe somebody else needs a summer girl," Mandi said, her hands covered in rich dark topsoil and a black smudge across her nose.

"Naw, I don't think I could be a summer girl," Star announced, her hoop earrings wobbling as she spoke. "Too much work."

"Yeah, too much work," Carly parroted. "Just like planting flowers."

"This isn't work," Mandi argued. "This is fun."

Carly didn't reply right away but watched as Jena dug a hole and carefully placed in a geranium into the earth before filling it around with dirt.

"I'm hungry," Carly whined. "I don't wanna plant flowers anymore."

"We're almost done, and then I'll make dinner," Jena said.

"Noooo, right now."

Jena stared up at the pouting little girl. "How about a few crackers while you wait? Would you like some crackers?"

Carly nodded.

Standing, Jena brushed herself off and entered the house. She plucked the graham crackers from the cupboard and returned to the yard. Sitting Carly on one of the two picnic benches, she opened the box.

"Hey, what are you making for supper?" Star asked.

"Grilled chicken and a tossed salad."

"Yum."

"Want to stay for dinner?" Jena said, going back to her knees to finish the flower-planting project.

"Will your boss care if I stay?"

"I don't think so. He's not that kind of a guy. Besides, he doesn't get home until eight."

"Well, then, sure. I've got no plans tonight, other than to soak my tired feet. I must have walked ten miles today and filled out just as many applications."

Jena inserted the last of the geraniums into what would become a colorful border. She stood and stretched out a kink in her back. Carly began to cry for no other reason than the fact she was overtired. At three years old, she still needed an afternoon nap.

Taking the little girl by one of her dirt-covered hands, she led her to the hose and washed her off. Carly protested the entire time. Next came Mandi's turn for her grubby bare hands and feet to be hosed off. After that, Jena cleaned off the gardening tools and sent Mandi over to Mrs. Barlow's next door to return them. Jena had looked but couldn't find a hand spade and rake in the garage and basement—although she hadn't felt comfortable performing an in-depth search. It seemed easier to borrow them from kindly Mrs. Barlow.

Carly's whines and complaints suddenly became a raving tantrum. Carrying the kicking and screaming child into the house and upstairs, Jena managed to wash her red, tear-streaked face and change the little darling into her nightgown. Minutes later, Jena left her in her bedroom to finish her temper fit.

Star crossed her eyes. "I don't know how you stand it. I couldn't put up with a kid acting like that!"

"She's over-tired. She'll probably sack out up there." Jena glanced at her wristwatch. Five-thirty. That wasn't too terribly early. There was a good chance Carly would sleep through the night.

Just then, Mandi skipped into the house. Jena instructed her to go upstairs and change clothes, which she did without a single objection.

"Hey, Star, will you keep an eye on things while I run over to my apartment and take a quick shower?"

"Um. . ." Her tall, willowy friend gave her a skeptical look. "I don't know, Jen. . ."

"It's quiet upstairs now. Carly probably passed out from exhaustion. Mandi's an angel, and it'll only take me twenty minutes. When I come back, I'll start the grill, and—"

"Okay, okay. Just make it quick."

"I will. I promise."

With that, Jena dashed out the back door and up to her apartment. The girls were safe and clean. She would be back in time to make a nice supper. What could go wrong?

six

Travis braked in front of his house when the gold, orange, and russet blooms of marigolds in front of the hedges caught his eye. When had he phoned the lawn and garden company? Did someone there call him? Life had been so hectic, he couldn't even remember.

Puzzled, he maneuvered his Lexus the rest of the way into his driveway and parked. Grabbing his briefcase off the passenger seat, he walked into the small courtyard that divided the house and garage. The girls' bikes were out, and Carly's favorite doll had been forgotten on the picnic table. Travis picked it up and noticed the pink buds of geraniums that now graced the edge of the house. Along the fence were several tall green leafy plants.

Since when does the lawn and garden company plant stuff without even asking what kind of flowers I want?

Miffed, he stalked into the house only to find a tall blond young woman standing in his kitchen wearing blue jeans and a light blue top that barely covered her tanned midsection.

"Who are you?" he asked, sounding brusque to his own ears. However, he didn't care for the ring in her navel. "Where's Jena?" He hoped she hadn't quit and left this person in charge. With her hair going every which way, she had a ditzy look about her.

"Uh-oh," the young lady said her blue eyes widening. "I just knew this was going to happen. . ."

"You knew what was going to happen?" Travis stepped into the kitchen.

44

"Well, lemme start by introducing myself. I'm Star."

Travis felt his frown deepen. *Star? What kind of name is that for a human being?*

"I'm Jena's friend," she continued, and as she spoke, Travis saw the braces on her teeth. "Jena said you wouldn't care if I was here. I'm just holding down the fort until she's done with her shower. She and the kids were planting flowers this afternoon, and—"

"Daddy!" Mandi zoomed into the kitchen, and Travis braced himself before she flung her arms around his waist.

"Hi, Baby," he said, bending over and kissing her. "Where's Carly?"

"She had a meltdown, and now she's asleep. I'm watching TV."

"Great. . .here, take Carly's doll with you."

"Okay, Daddy."

Mandi spun around on one bare foot and hightailed it out of the room. Straightening, he glanced back at. . .Star.

"So, you're one of Jena's friends, huh?"

"Yeah, she led me to Christ, and now she's discipling me. . . as well as trying to help me find a job."

"I see." Travis sort of understood the religious implications of the young woman's remark. His wife had been a born-again Christian, and she often spoke about "leading" someone "to Christ," although "discipling" was a new one on him. He presumed it meant Jena was some sort of mentor. "You're in college?"

"Yeah, I'm going to begin my junior year. But I don't go to the same school as Jena. I attend the University of Whitewater."

Travis blinked as Star tipped her head from side to side while she talked, and the hoops in her ears jangled. Nevertheless, he felt himself unwind. Things weren't so bad—so out of control as he'd first imagined.

"You said Jena and the girls planted flowers?"

"Yeah, that's why she needed the shower. It's hot, and she got kind of sweaty, you know?"

Exiting the room, Travis rolled his eyes. "Sweaty" was really more than he wanted to know. He traipsed into his office, a room with mahogany paneling and leaded glass-paned doors.

Setting his briefcase on a nearby armchair, he spied some envelopes stacked on the corner of his desk and figured Jena had put today's mail there. He lifted the small pile and rummaged through it. Hearing the back door open and close, he deduced that either Star left or Jena returned. He realized the latter had occurred when strains of female voices reached his ears.

Moments later, he heard footsteps and glanced up from the mail. Jena gave him a smile. Her tangerine-blond hair appeared a deeper color since it was still wet, and she had secured it in the back of her head with one of those plastic pinchy-comb things his sister used to leave all over the house.

"You're home early."

"Yeah, I've been known to do that every so often." Travis briefly noted the white t-shirt and tan straight skirt she wore. He also noticed her bare feet.

"I'm getting ready to light the grill."

"How come?"

"So I can cook the chicken that has been marinating all afternoon."

Travis pursed his lips and nodded. He thought about asking her if she'd cater Thursday night's dinner party but hesitated.

"Carly's sleeping," Jena said.

"I heard. Mandi told me."

"She was exhausted beyond reason."

Travis nodded. "That happens sometimes when she doesn't get a nap."

"So I've discovered."

He grinned at the quip.

"I hope you don't mind that my friend Mary Star came to visit me."

"Mary Star?" With the prefix, the name sounded a little more normal. "No, I don't mind. But what made you decide to plant flowers?"

"I saw an ad in the paper this morning promoting a big sale at a nearby garden center." Jena casually leaned against the doorframe. "I thought it would be fun for the girls to plant flowers, water them, and watch them grow and bloom all summer. You know. . .give them a sense of accomplishment. So after Mandi's swimming lesson, we went over and bought some flowers."

"Okay." Travis decided "a sense of accomplishment" was probably worth some flowers. "How much do I owe you?"

"I've got the receipt in my purse. I'll give it to you later." With that, she pushed off the door and headed for the kitchen.

"Jena," Travis called, wearing a smirk, "get back here."

She complied, but the innocent expression she mustered didn't work.

Travis crossed his arms. "Jena, you forget that I know this old female trick of diversion. Now, I'm not going to get angry. Just tell me how much I owe you."

"Eighty-nine dollars and ninety-four cents," she blurted. "In addition to the flowers, I bought some tomato plants and bags of topsoil."

Travis wanted to laugh. That was a whole lot less than the cost of his usual lawn and garden company. "I'll write you a check tonight."

"Okay," she replied, but her face was a bright shade of pink.

She made off for the kitchen again, and this time Travis couldn't contain his chuckles.

✿

"Was he mad?" Star wanted to know.

"No, of course he wasn't mad." Jena tried not to audibly expel her sigh of relief.

"What can I do to help with dinner?"

"Want to put the salad together for me?"

"Sure, I can do that."

Jena laughed at the understatement. Her friend had a flair for the culinary arts and hoped to operate her own restaurant someday. Walking to the fridge, Jena pulled out the lettuce, a tomato, and scallions and handed them off to Star.

"Jena, I'll light the grill," Travis said, giving her a start as he strode through the kitchen. "You shouldn't barbecue without shoes on. So unless you want me to burn the chicken, you'd better find something to put on your feet."

He marched out of the house, and Jena saluted in his wake. She looked over at Star who laughed at her antics.

"He's a hunk," she said.

"Yeah, and he knows it too," Jena whispered in case Mandi was within earshot. "But I have to say he's been very nice so far. A little bossy, but nice."

"A good-looking guy like him. . .a lawyer too. . .I'll bet he's got a line of women waiting to go out with him."

Jena nodded. The same thought had crossed her mind. But from what Mrs. Barlow said, Travis Larson was a family man through and through. Of course that didn't mean he wouldn't have an occasional date. In fact, Jena had a hunch he would ask her to baby-sit later than eight o'clock once Friday and Saturday night rolled around.

"Jena, come out here, will you?" Travis's deep voice boomed through the kitchen.

"Orders from headquarters," Star murmured with a laugh.

Jena had to chuckle as she walked outside. "What's up?"

she asked Travis who was busy pouring lighter fluid onto the charcoal.

"I've got a big favor to ask you."

"You've got a date and want me to stay late one night."

"*Urrrnt,* you're wrong," Travis replied, sounding like a game show host. He flashed her a captivating smile.

Must be a serious favor, she thought. *He's turning on the charm.*

"Unbeknownst to me, until late this afternoon, Craig Duncan, one of my partners, invited a prospective client to dinner on Thursday night. . .here. To my house."

"Oh. . ." Jena thought it awfully presumptuous of his business partner to do such a thing but refrained from saying so.

"Anyway, this client is Isabella Minniati. Ever heard of her?"

Jena shook her head.

"Well, she's a top executive for the Milwaukee Mavericks."

"Who?"

"It's an indoor football team."

Jena hoped she appeared impressed for propriety's sake. In truth, she wasn't crazy about football—outdoor or indoor.

"My firm is vying for the position of the Mavericks' corporate attorneys. Bella, that's her nickname, just found out she's expecting a baby, so Craig decided my house would be a cozy little backdrop for cinching this deal, seeing as I have two adorable daughters. . .and a summer girl who knows how to cook."

Jena's eyes widened with horror. "Me? Cook for somebody important?"

"Well, you cooked for me the last two days. What am I? A nobody?"

Jena noted his wounded expression and wondered if it were part of the presentation. "Of course you're not a nobody. I didn't mean that. I just. . .well, I like to cook, but I don't have a lot of confidence in my ability. . ."

Then suddenly it dawned on her. "Star. Star's a great cook! And she needs a job." She tipped her head. "Are you willing to pay extra for this?"

"Absolutely. Name your price."

"Um. . ." Jena was stumped. She hadn't a clue as to how much the job should pay. Fifty dollars? How much did cooks make an hour?

"Tell you what; I'll pay you each a hundred bucks. . .plus expenses."

"A hundred bucks each?" she repeated. "Hey, that sounds great." Jena thought the money would tide Star over until she found a real job and she, herself, could always use an extra one hundred dollars.

"So you'll do it? You and your friend Star?"

"I have to ask her, but if she agrees. . .sure, we'll do it!"

"Nothing fancy. Think homey."

"Like homemade vegetable soup and a loaf of home baked bread?"

"Yeah," Travis said with a pleased grin. "Like that."

"Well. . ." Jena put her hands on her hips and glanced at the blue, cloudless sky. "In that case, we'd better pray a cold front blows through. I have no intentions of slaving over a hot stove in ninety degree weather."

Striking a match and igniting the charcoal in the grill, Travis smiled and stepped back from the flames. "Jena, I don't care what kind of food you prepare. Just make it homey and impress Bella."

"Star and I will certainly do our best," she replied.

"That's all I ask."

Pivoting on the ball of her bare foot, Jena reentered the house, hoping Star was as receptive to Travis's idea as she had been.

seven

Jena and Star spent much of the next day planning and preparing for Thursday night's homey dinner. But when the day arrived, it was too hot to make the soup and bread they had selected, so they quickly changed the menu to steaks on the grill and seven-layer salad. Jena phoned Travis at work, and he gave his approval.

"I think everything's ready," Jena announced, entering the kitchen where Star put the finishing touches on the salad. "Now that's how I like to eat my vegetables." She gazed at the bacon bits Star sprinkled on top of the shredded cheddar cheese. "It looks fabulous."

"Thanks." Star beamed. "This is one of my summer specialties."

"I can tell."

At that moment, Jena glanced out the kitchen's picture window and spied the top of Mrs. Barlow's snowy-white head. Half a minute later, a knock sounded on the back door.

"Come on in," Jena called.

The older woman stepped into the back hall carrying a small cardboard box. "After you told me how the two of you have been fussing, I wanted to help, so I baked a rhubarb pie this afternoon."

"In this heat?" Star placed her cold soda bottle against her temple.

"Oh, it's not that hot." Mrs. Barlow's green eyes snapped with amusement. "Besides, a cold front is coming through tonight. Anyway," she said, looking at Jena, "the pie just came out of the oven, and I figure by the time Travis and his guests

51

are done eating dinner, it should be cooled enough to slice and serve with a scoop of vanilla ice cream."

With her hands in oven mitts, she extracted the pie from the box. Then she pulled out a round container of ice cream.

"Thanks, Mrs. Barlow." Jena took the frozen treat and set it inside the freezer. While she had planned to serve cheesecake for dessert, the rhubarb pie and ice cream sounded ever so much more "homey"—especially since Jena had used a no-bake boxed recipe.

Suddenly, Mandi came dashing into the kitchen. "Miss Jena, can you tell Carly to be quiet? She's crying, and I can't hear the TV."

"Why is she crying?"

Mandi shrugged. "I don't know. Come see. Make her stop it."

"All right. . ."

The six year old ran out of the kitchen. Jena followed, and reaching the den, she paused at one of its two doorways. Carly lay on the red and blue plaid sofa, whimpering.

Jena frowned as concern surged through her. "What's wrong, Carly? What's the matter?"

Sitting on the couch, she pulled the three-year-old onto her lap. Carly quieted and snuggled into her arms. Jena rocked her, and not to be left out, Mandi bounded onto the sofa and slipped her arm around Jena's, leaning her blond head on Jena's arm.

Mrs. Barlow's tall, broad-shouldered frame appeared at the doorway. She folded her arms and shook her head, smiling. "You're mother material if I ever saw it."

Jena smiled. "Well, I want to be a mother. . .someday."

She peered down at Mandi who regarded her with curiosity.

"How come you're not a mom now?" she asked.

"Because I'm not married. I have to find a husband first."

"Hey, I got it!" she cried, popping upright. "You could marry my daddy, and then you'd be our mom."

Jena felt her face begin to flame. She'd walked right into that one. "God has to find me a husband."

"That's right. It can't be little Miss Mandi Larson," the older woman said with a broad grin.

The girl pouted, and her brown eyes shifted from Mrs. Barlow to Jena. "Could Carly and me just pretend you're our mom?"

"Yeah," Carly murmured, "just p'tend."

"I don't think that's a good idea," Jena told them. She didn't want to start something she couldn't finish. Besides, she wasn't Travis Larson's type. She had seen pictures of his deceased wife, and the woman had been model gorgeous, slim figure, clear complexion—not a freckle face like Jena. Moreover, she sensed from the various photos she'd viewed that Meg Larson had been trendy and modern—not old-fashioned, which was more Jena's style. On the flipside, Travis Larson wasn't the sort of man who would capture Jena's interest. Ever since she moved to Wisconsin, she had been praying for a husband in the ministry—a missionary, a pastor. A lawyer wasn't even a consideration. "I'm just your summer lady, remember?"

"Good," Mandi said, curling up beside her once more. "Then summer's never gonna end."

"Of course it is, Silly." After a roll of her eyes, Jena gazed at Mrs. Barlow. "These two act like they're starving for affection."

"I don't think it's an act, Dear."

Jena felt a tiny piece of her heart tear. . .until she remembered seeing their father kiss and hug the girls. "Travis gives them affection."

"But it's not quite the same as a mother's tender nurturing. And, while you're not a mother per se, you have a motherly way about you. That's why I knew you'd be perfect for this job."

Jena smiled and glanced down at Carly whose eyes were closing off to sleep. Next, she peered at Mandi who had once again been absorbed by *Anne of Green Gables* on the television.

"Hey, Jen," Star said, entering the den, "your boss just got home, and a couple of other cars pulled up in front of the house. I can only assume his guests have arrived too."

"I'm going to leave," Mrs. Barlow said, giving Star a hug and blowing a kiss to Jena. "You're both going to do fine tonight. Travis is lucky to have you helping him out."

"Thanks for the pie," Jena called after her.

She turned and waved

Gathering Carly, Jena stood. "You know, this little girl feels awfully warm. What if I have to mind a sick child tonight? Will you be okay?"

"Sure. . .everything's basically done."

Star's confidence caused Jena to relax a bit.

"Daddy!" Mandi cried, jumping off the couch and running toward him with arms outstretched.

Travis met his oldest in the living room and swooped her up into his arms as his guests traipsed in through the front door. Smiling like a proud papa, he and Mandi greeted the two couples. Then he glanced toward the den as if looking for Carly, and Jena seized the moment to wave him over.

"I'm going back into the kitchen." Star spun on her heel and exited out of the den's second doorway.

Jena watched as her friend made her way through the dining room. Glancing into the living room once more, she stepped toward the other door and watched Travis's approach.

"Are we ready?" he asked, rubbing his palms together. Behind him, Jena could hear a woman exclaiming over Mandi.

"Well, yes. . .food-wise we're set. But I'm afraid we might have a sick little girl on our hands." She nodded at Carly whose head rested against Jena's shoulder.

Travis gave his daughter a dramatic frown, intended to make her grin. Then he put a hand over her forehead. "She's got a fever." A worry line formed above his dark brow. "Did you give her anything yet?"

She shook her head. "I just noticed how warm she felt a few minutes ago."

"Hmm…well, if she's not better by tomorrow morning, I'll call Dr. Becker, the girls' pediatrician. In the meantime, there's medicine upstairs in the linen closet."

"Great. I'll go get it."

"And I'll introduce my youngest daughter to our guests." Travis held his arms out to Carly, but she whimpered and buried her head deeper into Jena's chest.

"Carly!" Jena couldn't believe the child refused her father. Usually she was as excited to see him as Mandi.

"Oooh, you little heartbreaker." Travis tickled his daughter; however, Carly yelped and clung tighter to Jena.

"I think she's sicker than we first believed."

Travis narrowed his gaze. "I think she just knows which one of us is going to spoil her." Grinning, he winked at Jena.

She smiled back, but her heart suddenly beat in the strangest way. Maybe she was coming down with something too.

"Travis, is this your wife?"

Wide-eyed, Jena glanced at the doorway in time to see a slim woman with white-blond hair enter the room. Clad in a fitted black, sleeveless dress, she carried herself with an air of confidence.

"Hi," she said, "I'm Isabella Minniati. It's a pleasure to meet you. And who's this?" She sidestepped Travis to peer at Carly. "What an adorable little girl!"

Carly turned her face away.

"She's not feeling well," Jena tried to explain, "and I'm not—"

"Oh, what a shame," Isabella declared, touching the top of Carly's blond head. "Yes, she is a bit warm."

"Bella, this is Jena," Travis began. "She's my sum—"

"She's lovely, Trav," the woman cut in, whirling around to face him. "When I saw the two of you together in here and that darling child in your wife's arms, well, I. . .well, it was picture-perfect. You make a charming couple!"

Jena's jaw dropped, and she stared at Travis who rolled his eyes and shook his head just as two men strode into the room.

"Honey, this is Travis's wife, Jena," Isabella said to the husky man in a white polo shirt and dark slacks.

"A pleasure to meet you," he said with a genuine smile and a nod of his ebony head. "I'm Joe Minniati."

Jena forced a small smile and repositioned Carly in her arms. She looked back at Travis who was conversing with another man who appeared to be in his early sixties.

"Their little girl is sick," Bella went on.

"What a shame."

"So when did you and Travis get married? Poor Travis has been a single dad for so long." Bella pointed a well-manicured finger at him and laughed. "You needed a wife. You were getting awfully grumpy!"

"He certainly was!" the older man said.

He strode toward her, and Jena inadvertently took a step backwards, but he halted her process by placing his hands on her shoulders. "Great to see you again, Jena," he told her, batting one eye. Oddly, this wink didn't have the same affect on her that Travis's had earlier. "Well, folks," he said turning to face the Minniatis, "let's leave Jena to do her motherly thing and put her sick child to bed. Then we'll eat. Right, Trav? Jena's prepared a homey meal for us to enjoy. She's the picture of domesticity."

With that, he ushered the others into the living room, and Jena glanced at Travis.

"What in the world. . .?"

"I'm so sorry. We've traumatized you, haven't we?"

"Well, no. . .not traumatized exactly."

"Not to worry. I'll take care of everything." He swallowed hard. "After I throttle my partner. I bet I could get off with the insanity plea."

Jena ignored the quip. "That man with the bushy white hair. . .he's your partner?"

Travis's features softened. "Right. His name is Craig Duncan. He's senior partner at my firm." He shook his head and took several steps in her direction. "Look, Jena, I'll straighten things out. I promise. Craig's not thinking like a normal person right now. He's so desperate to sign this deal with Bella, he'd beg, borrow, and steal if he had to. But, instead, he's letting her believe a lie because. . .well, she obviously likes the idea that you and I are married."

Jena felt her face heating up at the implication.

"Again, I apologize." Travis ran a hand through his hair, a nervous gesture if Jena ever saw one. "Don't get mad and quit on me. . .please."

"Don't worry. I have no intention of quitting."

He expelled a weary-sounding sigh. "Good. That's the last thing I need."

Jena gazed down at Carly, deciding this was her chance to change a most uncomfortable subject. "I guess I should go tend to little one here. What kind of medicine am I looking for upstairs in the linen closet?"

"It's a bottle of children's fever reducer. Give her two tablets. I'll send Mandi up, and she can get in her pajamas. Meanwhile, I'll clear up the misunderstanding down here."

"Okay." That sounded like as good a plan as any. "Star's in the kitchen, and she'll put the steaks on the grill whenever you tell her to. The meat will only take a few minutes."

Travis nodded.

With Carly asleep in her arms, Jena felt as though her limbs might give out. Nevertheless, she marched purposely out of the den, making her escape to the second floor.

eight

With Carly sleeping and Mandi settled in for the night, Jena strode down the carpeted hallway, heading for the stairs. She hoped Star fared all right in the kitchen without her. Reaching the top of the stairwell, Jena paused, hearing footfalls ascending at a rapid pace. A heartbeat later, Travis rounded the landing and took the next flight two steps at a time, nearly colliding with Jena as he reached the second floor.

He caught himself in time and backed up. "Sorry 'bout that."

She gave him a forgiving grin. "That's okay."

"Are the girls sleeping?"

"Carly is, and Mandi's almost there."

"Good." He raked a hand through his dark brown hair. "We've got a problem."

"What is it?" Jena asked with a frown. "Did Star burn the steaks?"

"No, no, nothing like that." Travis drew in a deep breath. "You see. . .there hasn't been a good time for me to straighten out the matter of you being my summer girl and not my wife. I'd have to practically call Craig a liar in front of the Minniatis, and I can't do that."

Jena started to protest, but Travis held up a forestalling hand.

"He told Bella and Joe that you and I went to Paris for our honeymoon."

"No, he didn't!" she eked out an incredulous note.

58

"Shhh. . ." He glanced over his shoulder. "Yeah, he did. Bella asked to see our wedding pictures, and Craig said we haven't gotten them back from the photographer yet."

Jena stood there, gaping at him. "So now what?"

"Well, I wondered if you'd. . .well, if you'd play along."

"No!"

"Just for tonight."

"Absolutely not!" She folded her arms and prayed she looked adamant because her insides were quivering with sudden anxiety.

"You'll probably never see these people again, Jena."

"I can't lie. . ."

"You won't have to. You don't have to say a word. Just be polite and follow my lead."

"Travis, if I agree to this pretense, it's a lie."

Putting his forefinger to his lips, he glanced over the stairwell wall. "Jena, I'll give you and Star five hundred bucks each if you help me out."

"I can't be bought."

Travis smirked. "Your friend can. Star thinks this whole thing is hilarious, and she agreed to my offer."

"Then tell your guest that Star's your wife."

"Too late now." Travis stepped up to the landing, causing Jena to retreat. Taking hold of her elbow, he led her a few feet away so they wouldn't be overheard below. "Listen, it's for a few hours, Jena. That's all. Pretend you're an actress at your college performing in a play. . ."

She raised a dubious brow. "Comedy, or Shakespearean tragedy?"

Travis chuckled. "I think it's a little of both. But hopefully none of us will die at the end." He gave her a charming smile that made Jena's face flush. "Say yes. Please? This deal's important to my law firm."

Jena didn't feel right about being part of such deception. But, on the other hand, she didn't want to be the one responsible for his firm losing a big contract. Perhaps if she went along with this, she could somehow bring the truth to light, without publicly embarrassing Travis's partner.

"What's the verdict, Jen?"

Jen? She swallowed her surprise and continued her struggle with indecision.

Unfortunately, he interpreted her silence as acquiescence and propelled her toward the stairs.

"Bella's tired," he said in hushed tones. "This dinner won't last long. It'll be the easiest five hundred dollars you ever made."

"You don't have to pay me."

"Of course I do."

"No, I wouldn't feel right about it."

They reached the bottom stairs and strode to the living room.

"We'll discuss the matter later. . .Dear."

Jena's jaw dropped in indignation; however, she managed a recovery before they made their entrance.

"Well, here they are," Craig Duncan said, standing from the delicately patterned green and mauve sofa on which he'd been sitting. "Hope everything's okay, Trav."

Jena perceived the subtle warning in the older man's tone, and she felt suddenly sorry for Travis. True, she hadn't liked her boss much the day she first met him. But over the course of the last few days, it hadn't been difficult to see that he adored his daughters, and much could be said for a guy who loved his kids as much as Travis Larson did his. It made Jena wish her father had been as doting.

"Everything's fine," Jena shocked herself by replying. Then, seeing as she was on a roll, she decided to go for broke. "I hope I didn't appear rude, but with Carly sick and all. . ."

"Rude? Absolutely not!" Bella said from several feet away in the love seat beside her husband. "Your stepdaughter is more important than guests."

"I didn't even realize she had a fever until just before Travis got home."

"No need to explain," Bella insisted with a warm smile.

Jena felt a pinch of guilt for duping the woman. For some reason, she rather liked Bella Minniati.

"Now, who's in your kitchen cooking?" Bella asked before taking a sip of her iced tea.

"No one," Craig blurted. "Jena is just a fabulous home-maker all the way around. Isn't that right, Jena?"

"Well, usually. . .yes," she answered with an inward chuckle, thinking this acting stuff was kind of fun. But she had to laugh outright at the curious stare Travis gave her. Nevertheless, she saw an opportunity here for Star to get a summer job and chose to nab it. She turned to Bella. "I asked a friend to help me tonight. She's a great cook and. . .well, she'd make a terrific caterer. So I said she could practice on us."

Craig Duncan nearly choked on his beverage.

"But you won't be sorry, I promise."

"I'm sure you're right," Bella said glancing at Craig, then back to Jena. "And it so happens that I'm holding a garden tea party next month, and I'm in need of a caterer. Perhaps your friend would be interested in the position."

"Yeah, maybe she would be. Would you like to meet her? I'm going into the kitchen right now to make sure every-thing's ready. Want to come along?"

"I'd love to."

"I'll come along too," said the petite older woman who had been sitting next to Craig. Wearing a red cotton short-sleeved sweater, white linen pants, and coordinating accent jewelry, her regal bearing made it known that she identified with soci-ety's upper crust.

"What do you want in the kitchen, Miriam?" Craig's frosty, bushy brows almost touched the bridge of his nose as he frowned.

"I'm going to need a caterer for Samantha's bridal shower."

"Oh, right. I forgot about that." Craig rolled his eyes and waved his wife on.

Flanked by two obviously wealthy women, Jena refused to feel intimidated as they ambled to the kitchen. God wasn't impressed by a person's wealth; He saw the heart. . .and so did Jena, or at least she tried to.

"I just adore blue and white kitchens," Bella exclaimed as they entered the room. "Don't you Miriam?" Before the woman could reply, Bella added, "Did you decorate this yourself, Jena?"

"No, I didn't. . ."

Standing next to Star, she quickly changed the subject and made the introductions.

"I mentioned that you were thinking of starting your own catering business, like we discussed this afternoon." That wasn't a lie, either. Jena had listened patiently to Star ramble on about wanting to run her own restaurant business someday and catering was sort of like a restaurant business. "Mrs. Duncan and Mrs. Minniati might be interested in hiring you this summer."

"Oh?" A light flickered in Star's blue eyes as understanding set in. "Oh! Oh, yeah. . .my own catering business."

"Are you experienced?" Mrs. Duncan asked. "You look awfully young."

"I'm entering my junior year of college. I'm twenty-two. So, yeah, I'm young. But I do have experience."

Jena smiled as her friend rattled off all the school functions she helped cater at Whitewater, including two alumni balls.

Bella Minniati looked impressed. "Do you work alone?"

"Usually, but I can find help if the guest list is too large to manage myself."

"You seem quite capable. I'll bet you could handle my garden tea party single-handedly." Bella tipped her head, and her brown eyes darkened. "Let's talk business. How much do you charge?"

Jena glanced toward the entryway and saw that Travis had entered the room. With one hand on his hip, the other dangled next to his head as he leaned against the doorframe. He watched the transaction with interest.

"Okay, I have to claim ignorance here," Star said raising her hands as if in surrender. "I have no idea what caterers charge." She extended her hand, indicating to Travis. "He's paying me five hundred dollars for tonight."

"Five hundred dollars?" Bella looked aghast. "I can do better than that." Turning to Travis, she said, "You cheapskate."

"Hey, now, didn't you hear Jena?" He countered with a good-natured smirk. "Star's practicing on us tonight."

Bella gave him a doubtful glare and turned back to Star. "Another catering service quoted me a price of close to twenty-five hundred. Will you do it for a thousand dollars plus expenses?"

"Sure!"

Jena grinned at Star's enthusiasm before chancing a look at Travis. His expression said he found this entire incident quite amusing. His gaze eventually found hers, and he pushed himself off the side of the doorway and headed in Jena's direction.

"If we don't get those steaks going," he said, "Star will have to cook in the dark."

Jena gave him a nod. "Right."

Pivoting, she strode to the refrigerator, opened the door, and found the meat marinating on a baking sheet.

"Oh, now, Jena, don't go doing my job for me," Star said,

crossing the kitchen. "Mrs. Duncan, may I call you tomorrow so we can finish working out the details of your daughter's shower?"

"Of course, Dear. And, if this pans out, I have a friend who needs a caterer on the third of July at the yacht club." The woman smiled. "You may need help with that one."

"No problem." Star glanced at Jena. "Right?"

"Right."

"Ah, wait a second here," Travis cut in, giving Jena a pointed look. "We're going to have to discuss this matter of you moonlighting as Star's hired help. I don't know if I—"

"Oh, Travis, honestly!" Bella exclaimed with a laugh. "If it's appearances you're worried about, no one is going to care that your wife is helping her friend's business get off the ground. I think it's quite admirable. Star is working her way through school, and Jena wants to assist her."

Little does she know I'm working my way through college too.

Travis's gaze shifted between the two women, but it came to rest on Jena. She knew that he didn't want anything to interfere with her job as his summer girl, but of course, Bella had been purposely misguided, and so she'd drawn another conclusion.

As they stood there, regarding each other, Jena thought he appeared chagrined, and while she wanted to laugh, she instead put on her sweetest most wifely expression. . .whatever that was.

"We'll discuss it later. Not a problem. There are other people besides me who want to help Star out."

A slow smile spread across Bella's face. "You're a doll, Jena." She turned to leave the kitchen but paused to give Travis a rap in his midsection. "She's too good for you, Larson."

Travis narrowed his gaze, and once Bella was out of earshot, he said, "I can't stand that woman."

"Really?" Jena lifted the seven-layer salad from the fridge.

"That's a shame. I like her."

"That's because you're a nice person so you think everyone is nice." Travis came up behind her and took the rectangular glass pan out of her hands.

"I didn't think you were nice. . .at first."

Depositing the dish into its fitted serving basket, Travis shot her a curious glance. "We'll have to discuss that later, too," he said, carrying the salad to the dining room.

nine

Jena hurried to set two more places at the table, one for herself and the other for Star. She suspected it wasn't proper etiquette to have hired help eat with society's upper echelons, but Jena figured that since she'd been coerced into this farce of playing Travis's wife for the next couple of hours, she could invite whomever she pleased to dinner.

Back in the kitchen, Star sliced the individual tenderloins into succulent strips so that there would be enough for everyone. She arranged the meat on a shiny silver meat platter, then carried it into the dining room. Jena followed.

"We're ready."

"Great." Nervous flutters filled Jena's stomach.

Star frowned. "Are you sure you want me to eat in here? I feel kind of weird about it."

"How do you think I feel?"

"What's the next step up from weird?"

"Mortified."

"Yeah, that too."

Jena found the quip amusing. "Please, Star? I'd feel more comfortable with you at the table."

"Sure." A slow smile spread across the younger woman's face. "Whatever you say. . .Mrs. Larson. Hey, maybe since you're wife for the night, you ought to ask for the credit card."

"Oh, stop!"

Star laughed.

"Are we ready, ladies?" Travis asked, striding toward them with a purposeful expression. He lowered his voice. "I'd like to get this over with as soon as possible."

"Food's on the table," Jena said. "Call the guests in."

"No, I'd rather if you, being tonight's, um, hostess, would direct the guests to the table."

"Oh. . .well, if you say so." Jena gave her kinky strawberry-blond hair a self-conscious pat, although she felt glad she'd clipped it up off her perspiring neck.

"You look great," Travis muttered. "Just get them in here so they can eat and leave."

Something inside Jena wondered at the compliment. She looked great? Since when? Well, Travis was desperate. He'd most likely say anything so she would continue the acting.

She walked into the living room, where she politely interrupted the amicable chitchat. "Dinner's ready."

The guests ambled into the dining room, and once they were seated at the handsome cherry wood table, Travis reached for the plate of meat.

"We should ask the Lord's blessing. Travis, will you do the honors?" The words were out before Jena could stop them.

Travis shot her a wondering look. "Um. . .sure."

To her left, the Minniatis initiated handholding while they prayed, and Jena fought her smiles over the sight of Travis clasping Joe and Craig's hands. Funnier still was the perturbed expression on Craig's aged face.

They bowed their heads.

"God is great. God is good," Travis began. "Thank You, God, for this fud…Amen."

Bella collapsed against her husband's arm, laughing. "Oh, that was precious, Trav. Now pray for real."

His expression said he had prayed "for real." But to appease his guest of honor, he lowered his chin once more. Everyone followed suit.

"Thank You, God, for this food. And, um, thank You for

the hands that prepared this meal. . ."

Star squeezed Jena's hand. Jena squeezed back.

". . .Thank You for the good company here tonight. Bless us all. Amen."

Jena looked up as Travis reached for the meat platter again and passed it to his right.

"Are you one of those people who gets nervous when he has to pray in front of others?" Bella asked.

"Yeah," Travis replied in a crisp tone. He watched as Mrs. Duncan helped herself to the seven-layer salad and passed it to her husband.

"What about you, Jena?"

"Oh, she loves to pray," Star blurted.

Abashed, Jena simply confirmed her friend's statement with a tiny nod.

"She taught my girls to pray," Travis said, scooping salad onto his plate. Catching his blunder, he gazed across the table at Jena. "I mean our girls."

Jena felt her face begin to flame.

"Why didn't you teach them to pray?"

Watching the exchange, Jena noted that Bella didn't mean the question in a derogatory manner but asked it quite off-handedly as she sliced into her grilled beef.

"I, um, found it very hard to pray ever since. . .well, since Meg died." He passed the salad to Joe.

"Meg? Who's Meg?" Bella asked.

"That'd be Travis's sister," Craig stated.

"Meg was my wife," Travis countered, sounding as though his shadowy jaw was clenched as he spoke.

Craig laughed off his lie. "Oh, of course. Meg. Your wife. I'm terrible with names."

Bella looked aghast. "I'm. . .I'm so sorry Travis. I was under the impression you were divorced."

He shook his head. "Widowed."

"You're so young. Our age." Bella looked at her husband, then at Craig. "You said Travis was divorced."

"Me?" Craig appeared taken aback by the accusation. "I said no such thing."

"I beg your pardon," Joe cut in, "but you did indeed say Travis was divorced. It was right after we arrived here tonight."

"Oh, well." Craig waved his hand in the air, dismissing the issue. "I must have been thinking of my son. He's divorced."

Jena saw Mrs. Duncan's shocked expression, which she hid by staring down at her plate. Next Jena observed the Minniatis exchange curious glances, but all the while, her heart ached for Travis. Was he bitter with God for taking his beloved wife? Was he a Christian? Mrs. Barlow didn't think so. She had mentioned the many times she attempted to tell Travis about the love of Christ, although the older woman had informed Jena that Meg had been a believer.

"My humble apologies," Craig said, looking in Travis's direction before focusing on the Minniatis. "I've got a busy mind, and I meet so many people. Sometimes the names and faces just blur together."

"Perhaps you need your eyes checked. . .or your head examined." Bella gave him a tight smile.

Jena picked at her salad as the tension in the dining room mounted. Things weren't going well, but it was Craig Duncan's own fault for spouting off such lies tonight. Now Travis seemed completely disgusted, and Bella gave the impression of feeling just as aggravated.

She turned to Jena. "Your friend said you liked to pray. Is that true?"

"Yes. I'm a born-again Christian." She set down her fork. "I'm not always as faithful as I want to be, but I do enjoy conversing with the Lord."

"I know what you mean." The taut lines around Bella's perfectly shaped lips relaxed. "I'm a Christian too. So is Joe."

He grinned.

Jena smiled back.

"Jena's the one who led me to Christ," Star said. "I went to her church's Christmas program last year. At the end of the play, her pastor preached a short message about why we celebrate Christmas. It's 'cause of Christ. If He hadn't left Heaven and been born a man, there'd be no way for salvation and eternal life."

"Amen!" the Minniatis exclaimed in unison.

"I was one of the trained counselors milling about during the invitation," Jena further explained, recalling that snowy night, a week before Christmas. "I was matched with Star, and well, the rest is history."

"Now I'm like gum on Jena's shoe. She can't get rid of me."

"I'll vouch for that," Travis quipped.

Jena tossed him a quelling glare. However, she couldn't help a small grin. Then Star snorted with indignation, making things all the more funny.

To Jena's left, Bella laughed. "What church do you attend?"

"Countryside Community Church in Menomonee Falls."

Bella brought her chin back. "Way out there?"

Jena nodded out a reply.

"Well, Joe and I go to Parkside Baptist. It's not far from here. Would you and Travis like to join us this Sunday? Bring the girls," she said, looking at Travis now. "We'll all go out to lunch afterwards."

"Umm. . ."

Jena caught his eye and tried to shake her head without being obvious. "I have nursery duty on Sunday."

Travis feigned disappointment. "Aw, too bad."

"Can't you get out of it?" Bella persisted. "Trade Sundays with someone?"

"I think it's a great idea," Craig interjected. "You young couples can get better acquainted, and—"

"Us 'young couples' nothing!" Jena retorted. She'd had just about enough of this man and his endless fibs. It would do him good to go to church on Sunday. "I insist you and. . .and Miriam join us."

Mrs. Duncan appeared startled at Jena's familiar use of her given name.

Her husband, however, looked suddenly very irritated. His face reddened, making his white hair seem a shade lighter. "You insist?"

"Craig—"

"No, no, Travis. Don't try and defend her."

Bella gaped at the older man, and Jena felt as though she were a witness about to be cross-examined.

Craig's steely gray gaze bore into her. "You insist?"

Jena forced herself not to squirm; however, in the next moment it was as if the Lord revealed to her that she held the upper hand in this little game.

"Yes, I insist." she replied, lifting her chin. "You're coming and that's that."

"What?!"

She held his gaze, silently daring Craig Duncan to say one more word. If he did, Jena planned to confess the grand sham Craig so thoughtlessly instigated tonight. She'd probably lose her job, but. . .

The words of Queen Esther suddenly flittered through Jena's head. "If I perish, I perish."

"I think you've overstepped your bounds, young lady." Craig said. "No one's going to insist I do anything. Particularly you."

Jena turned to Bella who watched the exchange with an

expression somewhere between confusion and curiosity.

"There's something you need to know about tonight. I'm not—"

"Sunday morning it is!" Craig exclaimed, bringing his palm down on the table with a bang. "You know, Trav, I haven't been in church in years. This'll be refreshing."

Bella placed a hand on Jena's arm. "Ignore him. What did you want to tell me?"

"I'm not the person you think I am."

"Jena. . ."

Hearing what sounded like surprise mingled with hurt in Travis's voice, she looked across the table at him. "Travis, I can't lie anymore."

An almost wounded expression crossed his face, as if he'd been slapped, and for whatever the reason, Jena couldn't get herself to betray him. She searched her mind for a way to back out of what she'd begun to say.

"You see, I'm not as domestic as Craig has made me out to be." She stood and began to clear her place. Next, she took Star's plate. "I let you all believe I baked that rhubarb pie in the kitchen. But the truth is, our sweet neighbor Mrs. Barlow did."

Exiting the dining room, Jena caught Travis's look of relief.

ten

The sun was just beginning to set when the guests finally departed. The last three hours had seemed like a week to Travis. Even so, he glanced up Shorewood Boulevard and felt a moment's appreciation for the maroon and gray streaks painted across the sky. After a beep-beep from the Minniati's white SUV, he waved and forced a parting smile as the couple drove away.

"If Bella doesn't sign with us because of tonight," Craig muttered, "I'm taking that little upstart summer girl of yours to court for breech of contract."

"Don't be ridiculous. She never signed a thing. Where's your evidence?"

Craig grumbled. "I'll have Yolanda dig up something on her, and I'll go from there."

Travis laughed. "Good luck. Your chances of finding dirt on Jena are about as good as the chance of it snowing tonight." Unknotting his tie, he wished he had turned on the central air when he got home.

"Listen, that girl's got a lot of nerve insisting I go to church on Sunday morning."

"Yeah, well, I want to go to church about as much as you do." He waved away Craig's next remark. "I'll talk to Bella. I'll make up some excuse for tonight's. . .misunderstanding."

"No, you can't do that. Not unless she signs first."

Travis inhaled and willed himself to stay calm. He blew out a deep breath. "If we lose this contract, Craig, it's your fault. You might as well accept responsibility for it now. You started everything, and if I were Jena, I'd have socked you right in the nose."

"Then I would have had a good lawsuit, wouldn't I?" Craig chuckled, and his good-natured disposition returned. "Well, all in all, I think it was a productive evening."

Travis wanted to argue the point, but he felt too tired.

Craig walked around to the other side of the car. "See you tomorrow at the office, Trav."

"Right-o." He waved to Miriam through the window of the passenger side. She'd been waiting in cool comfort while he and Craig said their good-byes.

With his hands on his hips, Travis watched the Duncans' green Lincoln Town Car pull away from the curb and make its way up Prospect Avenue. Turning on his heel, he walked back to the house. One step inside the front door and he could hear Star's laughter over the din of the garbage disposal and running water. Next came Jena's reprimand.

"Mary Star Palmer! I cannot believe those words came out of your mouth! Just for that, I'm going to tell Tom. . ." Her voice trailed off.

Travis figured there was some big time teasing going on. Over the last couple of days, he'd gotten to know Star a little better. She seemed intelligent, but a little on the ditzy side, and she had a hankering for poking fun at Jena in a way that made Travis wonder why Jena put up with girl. He sighed. *Oh, well, what are friends for?*

He strode to the kitchen and entered just as Jena backed up to the doorway, dodging a flying wet dishrag. She stepped on his foot, and as a reactionary gesture, he set his hands on her waist to steady her. In doing so, he caught the soaking cloth in the shoulder.

Star's eyes grew as round as dessert plates. "Oops."

Jena swung around, and her face turned two shades of pink.

Travis held her blue-eyed gaze with his, as he balled the rag in his palm. Then without warning, he whipped it at Star. She yelped and jumped out of the way, but it splattered against her right elbow.

Jena whirled around and laughed. "That's what you get."

Star chuckled along before tossing the rag into the sink. "Yeah, I suppose so."

Smiling, Travis shook his head at the two of them. "You girls need to lighten up."

The sarcasm wasn't lost on either of them, and they replied with chagrined smiles.

"Listen, I'm sorry about tonight. Jena, I'm really sorry about tonight."

She lifted her shoulders in a quick up and down motion and resumed loading the dishwasher. Dressed in a white t-shirt and a crazy-patterned skirt and matching vest, she had ditched her sandals already, and Travis had to grin at the sight of her bare feet. She was as bad as his daughters.

"Guess I'll go up and check on Carly," he said, deciding he'd wait until Star left before talking to Jena about tonight.

"I did already." She glanced his way. "I don't think she has a fever anymore, and she's sound asleep."

"Oh, good." Travis looked from Jena to Star. "Then I guess I'll go up and change my shirt."

Chuckling at her guilty expression, he left the kitchen and took to the stairs with his usual two-at-a-time.

❧

"He always does that."

"Does what?"

Jena turned to Star. "He always runs up the steps like that. Practically shakes the whole house."

"Yeah, so?"

Jena shrugged. "Just something I noticed, that's all."

"Hmm. Well, I hope you're noticing the guy running up the steps too."

"Oh, Star, honestly! Will you stop it, already? I've told you—"

"I know. I know. You're waiting for God to bring the right man to you. You don't have to go looking. Our Heavenly Father will take care of it." Star shook her blond head. "But I'm telling you, Jena, I think He has."

"A lawyer? Yeah, right." Jena pointed towards the dining room and lowered her voice. "Look at his friends. I could never be one of those kinds of people. Besides, I don't think Travis is a Christian."

"If God saved me, He can save anybody!"

Jena didn't reply even though she agreed with Star. Nevertheless, Jena wished her friend would stop trying to pair her with Travis. It was most frustrating.

They finished cleaning the kitchen, and Jena started the dishwasher.

"You should see how he looks at you. I'm not kidding."

Jena moaned in aggravation. "Star! Drop it already!"

"All right, all right." The younger woman stepped back, her palms raised in surrender. "I will not say another word. Not one more thing."

"I'd get that in writing, Jen," Travis said, entering the room, checkbook in hand. He laughed at his own quip.

Jena prayed he hadn't heard what preceded it.

She watched as now, wearing a green Polo shirt and khaki trousers, he clicked his pen and began writing out a check.

"Just pay Star," Jena told him. "You don't owe me anything."

"Yes, I do, and I'm going to pay you." His voice sounded kind but adamant.

"No." Jena's tone was just as firm.

"She's in an argumentative mood tonight," Star said, throwing Jena a dubious glare.

"I need to repent for lying tonight, not get paid for it." She looked at Travis. "I don't want your money, and if you pay me, I'll rip up the check."

With that, she spun around and left the house. She walked across the small courtyard wondering why she felt so ornery. Normally, Star didn't get on her nerves, but tonight for some reason, Jena felt perturbed with her friend.

She reached her apartment's lower door and turned the knob.

"Jena. . ."

Travis's deep voice halted her, and she thought that maybe he was getting on her nerves too.

Slowly she turned around and watched as he came toward her. Star was right behind him.

"I'm leaving," she announced. "I'll call you tomorrow, Jena."

"Okay." She let her gaze follow Star out of the yard, then looked back at Travis, who now stood only a couple of feet away.

"If you're angry with me, I can understand why. But I promise I'll straighten everything out with Bella."

Nodding out a reply, Jena opened the door and stepped up into the hallway. She turned on the light, then brushed the hair that had fallen out its clip back off her face.

"If you won't take the five hundred dollars I promised you, fine. But you might as well take it. I'll see to it my law firm reimburses me." Travis put his foot up on the threshold and leaned forward on his knee. "It's money for school."

Jena wanted to tell him how accepting the money would make her feel. But she felt too embarrassed.

"Take it, Jena. I'll make out the check right now."

"I said I don't want it." She inched the door forward, only to have it connect with the toe of Travis's brown shoe. He didn't take the hint and move his foot, either.

"You earned it. Take the money."

"No, I didn't earn it. Don't say that."

"Why not?"

"Because it makes me feel. . .cheap."

There! She said it!

Jena drew in a calming breath and lifted her chin. She almost cracked a smile at Travis's stunned expression.

"I. . .I had no idea you felt that way. I'm very sorry. Nothing like that ever entered my head."

"It didn't really enter my head either. . .until you tried to pay me."

"My sincere apologies, Jena."

"All's forgiven. Let's just forget it, okay?"

"Okay."

He removed his foot, and she began to close the door, when Travis caught it before it met the latch.

"Yes?" She peeked around the door.

His brown eyes filled with apprehension. "You're not going to quit on me, are you?"

She rolled her eyes as a smile edged its way across her face. "No, I'm not going to quit on you." She must have told him that four times this week. "I do need the summer girl job, you know."

"Good." He took several steps backward, but he still wore a wary expression.

"I'm not going to quit on you," she reiterated. "I promise."

Halfway into the courtyard, he managed a cordial smile. "Good night."

"Good night."

On that, Jena closed the door, locked it, and ran up the steps—two-at-a-time.

eleven

The next morning, Travis awoke to the sweet smell of cinnamon, fresh bread, and coffee. By the time he'd showered, shaved, and dressed, the girls were at his bedroom door exclaiming over the fact that they'd made sweet rolls.

"Daddy, you have to come downstairs and eat breakfast now."

"Yeah, all right. . ." He gazed at Mandi through the mirror while knotting his tie. "You're awfully bossy for a six-year-old, know that?"

She gave him a sassy smile before climbing up on his bed. He could tell she had every intention of using it as trampoline.

"Hey, off the bed. No, don't jump. Get off."

She took a flying leap and landed on his back, causing him to lose his balance. He fell into his bureau, knocking over a couple of cologne bottles and a picture of Meg.

"Amanda Lyn Larson, what do you think you're doing?" Travis peeled off her arms from around his neck and swung her over his shoulder so that she hung upside down.

She giggled so hard her lanky body shook, and Travis tossed her onto the bed.

Some example I am. He shook his head at Carly who was in the process of mimicking her older sister.

"Don't do it," he warned her.

But, wearing an impish grin, Carly started jumping on his bed despite the words of caution. With each bounce, she jostled Mandi who laughed so hard she couldn't sit upright.

Travis snatched his youngest in midair. She giggled and he

79

tickled her, tossing her on the bed too. Then he tickled the both of them until they squealed and screamed, pleading for mercy.

"There." Holding them around their forearms, he brought them both to a standing position. "Now I'm the dad, and I say. . .no more jumping on the bed. Got it?"

"Tickle us again, Daddy," Carly said, a huge smile on her sweet, round face.

He gazed upward, shaking his head. So much for authority and influence. "Sorry, fun's over. I've got to be in court this morning. Here," he added, hoping to distract them, "Mandi, you carry my briefcase, and Carly, you carry my suit coat." He folded it in her arms so she wouldn't trip on it.

"Daddy, this is too heavy for me," Mandi declared, setting the attaché on the top of the steps.

Carly flung his jacket and followed her sister down the stairs. "Some help you two are."

Gathering his things, he made his way to the first floor. After a quick stop in his office, he entered the kitchen. Jena glanced at him, then did a double take, and he watched her gaze take in his appearance. Suddenly, he realized the tails of his shirt had come untucked, and his tie was askew.

"I'll have you know I was all spit 'n polished before my daughters attacked me." He combed his fingers through his hair in case it, too, had been mussed.

"I didn't say a word."

He caught her smirk. "You didn't have to."

Travis watched as Jena flitted around his kitchen in a yellow and white patterned jumper and white T-shirt. Her hair hung to her shoulders, and it looked like it was still wet from a shampoo. His gaze traveled down to her feet—which were bare, just has he expected. But today he noticed the berry colored polish on her toenails. And then he noticed that Jena had very pretty feet—as far as feet go—and she had nicely turned ankles too.

"I hope that you don't mind that I walk around your house barefoot."

"What?" Travis looked up, realized what she'd asked, and shook his head. "No, of course I don't mind. Why would I?"

"I don't know. Just thought I'd ask."

He ignored her curious expression and reached for a frosted cinnamon roll.

"Want a cup of coffee?"

"Yeah, thanks."

From the dishwasher, she pulled out his travel mug, held it up in question, and he nodded. Funny how quickly she learned his routine. Travis didn't particularly like sitting down to a formal breakfast. He wanted something to grab and go, and he enjoyed taking his coffee with him.

"Where'd the girls take off to?" he asked, watching Jena add cream and sugar to his brew.

She smiled. "I bought them each a little plastic watering can, and they're just outside giving our flowers a morning drink."

"Oh, good. That'll keep those two urchins busy for a few minutes."

Finishing off his sweet roll, he reached for another. He munched on it while observing Jena as she twisted on the lid of his stainless thermal mug. Her fingers were long and graceful, and a smattering of tiny brown freckles covered her capable hands and traveled up her arms. Before he could contain the thought, he wondered if her skin felt as soft as it appeared. . .

"Did I do something wrong?"

Travis swallowed the food in his mouth and met Jena's questioning stare. "No, why?"

"Well, I don't know, but. . ." Her freckled cheeks turned petal pink. ". . .you're looking at me kind of weird."

"Oh, sorry…"

He stuffed the rest of the cinnamon pastry into his mouth before he could contend that his appreciative glances had never been called "weird" before.

Jena handed him his mug. "Are you going to talk to Bella today?"

He sipped his coffee before answering. "I'll talk to her. . . soon."

"Today?"

Her eyes beseeched him, and Travis suddenly noted their unique color. A dark blue-gray—like the color of a summer sky before a storm.

"Travis?"

"Hmm?"

"Today? Are you going to speak with Bella today?"

"If I get a chance. . ." Travis tried to make his reply as vague as possible, knowing Craig would shoot him if he told Bella the truth before she signed the contract.

Jena, however, didn't look satisfied with the implied promise.

"Listen, don't worry." He touched her arm, a gesture of reassurance, but a tiny thrill passed through him when he learned her skin felt, indeed, quite soft. "I'll. . .I'll take care of it. I'll explain about last night, okay?"

A small worry line marred her auburn brow. "Are you feeling all right, Travis?"

"No! I think I've gone crazy!"

"Oh, is that all?" Jena laughed, breaking whatever spell he'd fallen under.

"You sound like your friend Star," he muttered, leaving the kitchen. If there was one thing in this world he abhorred, it was a sarcastic woman.

In his office, he straightened his clothes, combed his hair, grabbed his briefcase and suit coat, then made his way toward the back door.

"See you tonight," he said, walking through the kitchen.

"Bye, Travis. Have a good day."

Jena's soft voice plucked a chord in his heart, one he'd never heard or felt before—even when Meg was alive. Every day this week, with the exception of last night, he had felt like he'd entered some kind of storybook fantasy where everything was perfect and wonderful. It was a world where delicious smells wafted from the kitchen, laundry never piled up, and children were always clean and happy.

He shook himself. *I have gone crazy.*

~

Gazing out the window, Jena lifted her coffee cup to her lips and sipped. She saw Travis kiss Mandi and Carly goodbye before walking into the garage. He sure acted strange this morning. Maybe he just had a lot on his mind. She only wished Star hadn't put those silly thoughts in her head about Travis "looking at her" in some romantic way because she could almost swear that's what he did this morning.

The phone rang, and Jena moved to answer it where it was stationed on the wall near the back hall. "Larson residence."

"Is Travis gone?"

"Um, just leaving now. Who's calling please?"

A feminine laugh. "It's Bella Minniati. How're you this morning?"

"Fine. Thanks." Jena tried to tamp down the feeling of impending doom. "Do you need to speak with Travis? I'll try to catch him."

"No, no, I want to talk to you, Jena. I just don't want him in the vicinity while we converse."

That's what she was afraid of. *Oh, dear God. . .*

"Jena, I might be blond, but I'm not stupid. I could sense some odd undercurrent last night, and I want you to tell me what was going on. I think you were about to tell me while we were at the dinner table. Am I wrong?"

"No. . .but Travis said he'd rather be the one to discuss the matter with you."

"I see. Are you two having marital problems?"

"Oh, no, nothing like that."

"I didn't think so. You two are adorable together. But I thought I'd nip that suspicion in the bud."

Jena squeezed her eyes shut in a tight grimace.

"Well, I really don't want to wait for Travis to tell me. I'd like to hear it from you. I'm not trying to be nosey. I'm just. . . concerned."

"Oh, Bella, I really shouldn't be the one to tell you."

"But you will tell me, won't you? You're my sister in Christ, and I have a hunch whatever is going on involves me and this contract business."

"Yes, you're right. And that's why Travis needs to speak to you."

A long pause. "Jena, I'll tell you a piece of truth if you tell me a piece of truth. Deal?"

"Okay. . ." She didn't see another option out, other than to hang up on Bella and maybe ruin whatever hope remained of her signing with Travis's law firm.

"I've always thought that Travis was an okay guy. But now I actually like him since I met you and those two darling girls."

At the mention of Mandi and Carly, Jena went up on her tiptoes and glanced out the window to make sure they were all right. Seeing the little ones sitting inside their square, wooden sandbox near the fence, she returned her attention to the phone call.

"But I must say, Jena, I trust Craig Duncan about as much as I'd trust a rattlesnake. The man appears harmless enough, but I have a feeling he's got a venomous bite."

"Good analogy."

Bella's laugh was as smooth as expensive chocolate. "Thank you. I take it you agree?"

"Wholeheartedly. But, of course, it's none of my business."

"What? You're Travis's wife. Of course it's your business."

Jena's heart hammered in her chest. "Okay, my turn for a piece of truth. I'm not Travis's wife. I'm his summer girl."

"His what?"

"Summer girl. He hired me to take care of his kids for the summer."

"You're a nanny?"

"Well, yes, but, no. I hate that title. Except, I suppose that's what I am. . .for the summer." When there was no reply, Jena continued. "It was all Craig Duncan's doing. He lied, thinking that somehow our being married would impress you, and Travis didn't want to expose his rattlesnake partner in front of guests, so he begged me to go along with it for the night. Trust me, I didn't want to, but. . .well, I felt kind of sorry for Travis, being in that awkward position because of Mr. Duncan."

The silence at the other end was deafening. "Bella, please believe me when I say I'm so sorry for the pretense. My conscience bothered me into the wee hours of this morning."

"So am I correct in assuming that only the part about you and Travis being married is a lie?" Bella asked. "The girls are Travis's and he's a widower?"

"That's true." Jena felt like a two-ton weight had just been lifted off her shoulders. "And Star is a friend of mine, and she really needs a job for the summer. She's excited about the catering possibilities."

"I see."

"Bella, I'm so, so sorry."

"You're a Christian? That part's true?"

"Yes, but I probably don't seem like much of a testimony for Christ right now."

"On the contrary. I admire your tender spirit. I felt like you and I sort of connected last night." She paused. "Tell me. Is Travis a Christian?"

"I'm not sure."

"Mm. . .Joe and I wondered."

Jena heard the other woman inhale deeply.

"Tell you what," Bella began, "let's keep our Sunday morning date, shall we? I like you, I forgive you for your part in last night's charade, and I think those two girls are so scrumptious I could eat 'em up."

Jena smiled. "I agree. Mandi and Carly are sweeties. And, in Travis's defense, I have to say, he's a very loving father. He's also extremely generous. He's given me a car to use, he leaves me money for whatever the girls and I might need, he's polite and he doesn't talk down to me—which is pretty amazing considering he's a lawyer. . ."

Bella chuckled, sounding genuinely amused.

"I mean, I know all attorneys aren't arrogant," Jena promptly amended, "but I thought Travis was at first. I've learned he's really not."

"Okay, you sold me on his attributes." Bella laughed again. "I forgive Travis too."

"But I don't know if he'll want to come on Sunday."

"Hmm. Well, if he doesn't, then you can't very well bring him kicking and screaming. But I'd like you to come—and bring Mandi and Carly."

"Okay."

Jena nibbled her lower lip in consternation. Sunday was technically her day off. However, she didn't think Travis would mind her borrowing his daughters—

Unless, after he heard she'd blabbed the truth to Bella, he fired her first!

twelve

Travis loosened his tie as he drove back to that enchanted new world called home. He had called Jena on his cell phone and found she didn't need groceries or anything else. The girls had been fed and bathed and were now watching some Bible story video they had checked out at the library.

Bible story videos. . .they sure beat the kind of television Glenda used to watch. Pulling into the driveway, Travis parked and decided Meg would be pleased the girls were being introduced to the Bible. In fact, Meg would probably like Jena.

Travis walked through the yard, noting all the toys were put away. When Glenda was here, the place was such a disaster he'd be lucky if he didn't kill himself on the way to the back door. And the house. . . The house always looked as though Hurricanes Mandi and Carly had blown through every room.

What a change, he thought, entering the immaculate kitchen. He paused to inspect the fresh flowers in the center of the table.

"Hi, Daddy!" Mandi pranced into the kitchen, looking like a little princess in her pink nightie.

"Hi, Baby," Stooping, Travis hugged and kissed her. "Where's Carly?"

"Sleeping on the couch. She didn't have a nap today 'cuz Miss Jena took us to the beach. On the way back, we bought those," she said, pointing at the colorful bouquet. "Do you like 'em?"

"Yeah, they're pretty." Travis stood. "What'd you eat for supper?"

"The stuff Miss Star made yesterday."

Mandi said the name so fast that Travis didn't catch it. He frowned. "Mister? Mister who?"

"No, Daddy, Miss Star."

"Oh, is she here?"

Mandi shook her head.

Good. Travis had had such a hectic day that he didn't feel like dealing with Mary Star Palmer's antics tonight. All he wanted to do is change into his blue jeans and unwind in a lawn chair outside.

"Hi, Travis, did you have a good day?"

He smiled as Jena entered the room. "It was okay." He'd lost the Baily case, but that had been expected. Now came the appeals process. In two sweeping glances, he scrutinized Jena from head to barefooted toe. "You look about as pink as Mandi's nightgown."

"Yeah, I know." She examined her arms. "I took the girls to the beach today but didn't bring along enough sun screen. By Sunday, I'll be one giant freckle."

Travis grinned and stepped closer. "Did you wear that to the beach today?" he asked, noting she wore the same outfit as this morning.

"No, of course not." Confusion pooled in her blue eyes.

He smirked. "I just wondered since I've never seen you wear anything but a dress."

"Oh." She shrugged, still looking baffled.

No wonder Star goads her. Jena's awfully fun to tease.

Travis flashed a charming smile while brushing past her on the way to his office. Tossing his attaché case on a nearby chair, he flipped through the mail.

"Hey, Travis?"

"Hmm?" He glanced up to see Jena at the doorway.

"After the girls are sleeping, can I talk to you about something. . .something important?"

The trepidation in her voice put him on guard. Sitting on the corner of his desk, he set down the mail and folded his arms. "What's up?"

"I'd rather wait until Mandi and Carly are asleep to discuss it." She smiled. "But I'm not quitting, so don't get your hackles up. Although. . ." A worried little frown suddenly dipped her one eyebrow. ". . .you might not want me working for you when you hear what I have to say."

Travis wanted to hoot at the comment, but he refrained only because she seemed troubled. "Jena, I highly doubt there's anything you could tell me that would cause me to let you go. You're doing a great job. You've brought normalcy back to my home. In fact, after three years it finally feels like a home again."

"That's. . .that's nice to hear," she said with a pleased grin. "But just hold that thought until I get the girls to bed, okay?"

Travis chuckled and picked up the stack of bills and miscellaneous correspondence. "Okay."

❧

After reading Mandi a story, Jena turned out the light and proceeded to the first floor where she scouted around for Travis. She finally found him in the courtyard, stretched out on one of the two padded lounges and reading the newspaper as the sun began its nighttime descent.

"The girls are just about asleep."

"Great." Travis folded the paper in two and set it on his lap. He still wore today's white dress shirt, its sleeves rolled to elbows. He'd removed his tie and exchanged his classy trousers for faded blue jeans. "So what did you want to talk to me about?"

Jena sat down in one of the plastic lawn chairs. She'd been rehearsing this all day, but now when it came time to tell Travis about her confession, words suddenly escaped her.

"Did you wreck the car?"

Jena's eyes widened. "No!"

A small grin tugged at one corner of his mouth. "Did you nick it, bang it, or dent it, and now you're scared to tell me?"

"No." She couldn't help a chuckle. "That I wouldn't have trouble telling you."

"Oh, okay." He pursed his lips, appearing amused.

But he wouldn't be for long.

"Bella called this morning, right after you left," Jena blurted.

"Oh?" The tone of his voice hung between them like a threat.

With flutters dancing across her midsection, Jena crossed her leg and toyed with a small snag in her jumper. She swallowed hard. "Bella sensed that something was amiss last night and. . .well, I ended up telling her the entire truth."

Travis swiveled in the lounge chair, and glancing at him from beneath her lashes, Jena saw his navy and white athletic shoes when he set them on the cement ground. He leaned forward, his forearms on his knees, but his expression was indecipherable.

"What did Bella say?"

"She said she doesn't trust Craig Duncan."

"Oh, great." Travis ran a hand through his hair.

"But she likes you, and she still wants us to come Sunday. I told her I didn't know if you'd be willing to attend church, and she said in that case I should come without you and bring the girls." Jena cleared the sudden frog in her throat, spawned from Travis's penetrating gaze. "Sorry," she croaked.

"Anything else?"

She shook her head, sensing Travis's infuriation. But that's what she expected. Nevertheless, she felt the need to explain herself. "If I blew the big contract for your firm, I humbly apologize. On the other hand, I couldn't tell Bella a boldface lie. I mean, going along with things last night was one thing—"

Travis held out a forestalling palm. "Say no more. I understand."

"If you want to end my employment here—"

"No, no. . .I meant what I said earlier."

"Okay." She stood. "Well, it's after eight. . ."

"Fine. Consider yourself off duty."

He studied his clasped hands as he spoke, and Jena decided he was deep in thought—probably trying to figure out how to tell his pretentious partner that his summer girl had a big mouth.

"Travis, I know it's none of my business, but. . .well, I don't like Craig Duncan. I think Bella has an accurate opinion of the guy."

He glanced up at her, one eyebrow cocked. "You're right, Jena. It's none of your business."

Her breath caught in her throat. She felt like she'd just been slam-dunked. But in the next moment, she figured she had it coming. She'd been Travis Larson's employee for six days. She was the hired help and hardly entitled to pass judgment on his business partner.

"Sorry."

Jena crossed the courtyard and ran up to her apartment. She felt somehow wounded, she wanted to cry, and yet she believed in her heart she'd done the right thing this morning on the phone with Bella. She'd told the truth.

Deciding to drown her blues in a strong cup of java, she walked to the kitchen and opened the cupboard. Only then did she remember that the coffee was in Travis's kitchen.

With a frustrated groan, she closed the cupboard doors and ambled to her room. By the time she reached it, she'd made up her mind to walk to that little coffee shop she had seen on Oakland Avenue. Since the village of Shorewood was only one square mile, Jena figured she could walk there and back.

Moving to the dresser, she pulled out a pair of black walking shorts and put them on. She winced as they chafed her sunburned legs. Being more careful now, she removed her jumper and hung it in the closet, exchanging it for a short-sleeved cotton black shirt with sprays of tiny yellow, red, white, and lavender flowers. She layered it over the white tee she wore. After threading a belt through her shorts, Jena donned a pair of white sport socks and slid on her white athletic shoes. In the bathroom, she brushed her hair and glided a headband into place. She squirted lotion into the palm of one hand and gently applied it to her face. *I'm so pink I put Star's favorite shade of lipstick to shame.*

With a sigh, she figured there was nothing more she could do in the aftermath of a sunburn, and she slung her small purse over her shoulder and left the apartment. She felt relieved that Travis no longer sat in the courtyard. Taking a deep breath of the evening air, she felt herself begin to relax as she began her trek up Shorewood Boulevard.

❧

Up in his bedroom, Travis sat on the edge of the bed, mourning the framed picture of Meg that he found lying broken on his dresser. He knew just when it had happened too—this morning when Mandi had playfully jumped on him. He could buy another frame, that wasn't a problem, but somehow the shattered glass above his Meg's smiling face seemed like the final barrier between them. A ridiculous notion, of course, since his wife had been dead over three years now. Nevertheless, he couldn't explain away the sudden sense of permanence that enveloped him.

Meg wasn't coming back.

She was gone forever.

Sniffing back and swallowing the sorrow that crashed down

around him every so often, Travis stood and headed for his dresser again. In doing so, something caught his eye, and he glanced out the window.

Jena. . .

An undefined emotion twisted in his chest, and he had to fight the urge to holler out the window, "Wait! Don't go!"

She's not leaving for good, you idiot. She's probably just meeting some friends.

As Travis watched his summer girl walk up the boulevard, her tangerine-colored hair swinging just above her shoulders, he regretted being so terse with her earlier. True, he wasn't exactly thrilled that she'd told Bella the truth, but he also cringed at the thought of life without her. In one week's time, Jena had set his skewed world right again.

That's the Lord, Travis. See what the Lord can do?

The memory of Meg's voice rang in his ears, and he gazed at her photo again. She'd said those words a thousand times—whenever something good happened. "That's God." or "That's the Lord." On the other hand, when hard times hit, Meg said that was God too. "We'll rejoice in adversity, and God will see us through."

Travis shook his head and placed the picture in its damaged frame onto his dresser. Meg had been the ultimate Pollyanna if there ever was one. Every cloud had a silver lining and after every dark storm, there was a bright, beautiful rainbow. Meg had become a Christian shortly after Mandi's birth, and while she tried to get Travis to "see the Light," he'd never been interested enough to try to understand.

But there was one thing he now knew for certain: a Christian woman in his home, caring for his girls, was the difference between contentedness and catastrophe.

thirteen

Jena sat alone at a back table in the coffee house, flipping through the bridal magazine she'd purchased at the drugstore across the street. No sooner had she taken a sip of the hazelnut-flavored iced coffee than a young man approached her.

"Excuse me, but don't I know you?"

He stood as tall as a California redwood. After craning her neck to glimpse his face, Jena shook her head. "I don't think so. At least you don't look familiar to me."

"Did you go to Lakeview College in Watertown?"

"Why, yes." Jena smiled. "I still attend, actually. I'll be finishing up my last semester come fall."

"I'm Rusty McKenna," he said, folding his lanky frame into the chair across from her. Jena noted his auburn hair and thought his name was quite fitting.

"Nice to meet you. I'm Jena Calhoun."

He squinted, studying her face, then pointed a tapered finger at her. "You're the one I've seen around Mr. Larson's place."

"Yes, how did you know?"

"Because I live across the street—well sort of across the street. His place is at the dead end of Shorewood Boulevard, and we're two houses in from the corner."

"Oh." Jena gave him a polite smile.

"Are you a relative taking care of his kids?"

"No, Travis hired me to watch Mandi and Carly for the summer."

Rusty nodded out a reply, while Jena considered him. Long

and narrow with his nose and jaw jutting outward, there was an equine sort of look to his face. She wouldn't say he was "handsome," but he wasn't unattractive, either. He had fascinating eyes and an intelligent light shone from their hazel depths.

"What's your major?"

"Home Ec," Jena replied. "And yours?"

"Was. . .Pastoral Studies. I just graduated earlier this month."

"Congratulations!"

He beamed. "Thanks."

"So. . .you're going into the ministry?

Rusty nodded. "I feel I'm called to preach, but I just don't know where yet."

Hope bubbled up inside of Jena. *Is this the one, Lord?* She'd been praying for God to send her a husband, and she wasn't being that picky. She wanted a missionary. . .or a pastor.

Very discreetly, Jena closed the bridal magazine and set it face down on the table, beneath her handbag.

"So who's the blond I've seen over at the Larsons? She drives that older model Cavalier."

"Oh, that's Mary Star. She's become a friend of mine since accepting Christ last December."

"Oh, neat." Rusty bobbed his large head, his wide mouth pursed in thought. "You're both single, I take it."

"For the time being," Jena replied with a sassy grin.

Rusty chuckled. "Say, you want a lift back to the Larsons'? I'm leaving in a few minutes. I just need to say goodbye to a few of my friends. They're sitting up in front."

"Oh, sure. That'd be great. I'd love the ride home. Thanks."

Rusty stood with a parting smile and walked away while Jena tried to quell her excitement. *Oh, God, please let me know if this meeting was ordained by You.* Leaning sideways, she lifted the plastic shopping bag containing the analgesic lotion for her sunburned skin that she bought along with the magazine. Rolling up the publication, she stuffed it into the bag. Coffee in one hand, she slung her purse over her shoulder, trying not to wince, and gripped her purchases with the other. Then she made her way up the row of tables to where Rusty conversed with three other young men.

"Hey, guys, this is Jena," he said, as she approached.

She sent them each a polite smile, and they nodded back at her.

"She works for Mr. Larson across the street. . .remember, I prayed about somehow meeting that woman I told you guys about. Well. . ." He waggled a thumb in Jena's direction.

He prayed about meeting me? Jena's pulse quickened.

Meanwhile grins and exclamations emulated from his buddies. Jena felt her face flush scarlet. She took a sip of her iced coffee in an effort to conceal her chagrin.

"Listen, I've got an idea." Rusty turned to her. "How 'bout we go to the zoo tomorrow. Mark, here, will come with us, and you can ask your friend Mary Star to come along."

Jena mulled it over. Rusty probably wanted friends to accompany them so he wouldn't feel uncomfortable their first time out together. But there was just one problem.

"I'll have to take Mandi and Carly."

"Oh, sure, that's fine. We don't have anything against kids, do we, Mark?"

"Umm, I have things to do tomorrow. . ."

"You owe me one, Buddy."

Mark rolled his blue eyes and glanced across the table at his cronies. "Yeah, okay, but let's go in the morning. I've got stuff to get done in the afternoon."

"Deal." Rusty turned to Jena. "Okay with you?"

"Sure." She was up early and so were the girls. She didn't think Travis would care if they went to the zoo.

"Do you think Mary Star will agree to come along?"

"I can probably persuade her."

"Great." Rusty grinned at his friends. "Mary Star. . .what do think of that name, huh?"

They all shrugged.

Jena smiled. "She likes to be called Star for short."

One of his pals laughed. "Great. Her name matches the stars in Rus's eyes."

Rusty waved a hand at them, then looked at Jena. "Do you see stars in my eyes?"

Embarrassed, she raised her shoulders in a quick up and down motion.

"Listen, you guys, I'll see you later. I'm driving Jena home. Mark, I'll pick you up bright and early. . .let's say around eight."

"I'll be ready." His tone didn't sound very enthusiastic, but Rusty seemed oblivious to the fact.

"C'mon, Jena."

She followed him out of the coffee house and walked beside him up the street until they reached a light blue mini-van. Rusty pulled the keys out of his pocket and walked around to the driver's side. Once he'd climbed in behind the wheel, he popped the automatic lock, and Jena, juggling her coffee and drugstore purchases, opened the door.

"Nice night, isn't it?" he asked as she tried to gracefully seat herself in the van without spilling her coffee.

"Yeah, it's. . .nice." She managed to close the door, thinking Rusty should have helped her into the vehicle. Jena had several male acquaintances, whom she'd met at school, and they often went out together—girls and guys—as a group. Even in that platonic situation, one of the men would open the car doors for the ladies.

"Do you know Ben Talbot?" Jena asked.

"Yeah, I think so." Rusty started the engine. "Is he short and kind of going bald already?"

"Yeah. . ." Jena hadn't ever heard Ben described in such a negative light before. The guy had a heart of gold. "He's getting married in November to Denise Anderson. Do you know her?"

"No."

"Oh. . ."

It was then that Jena realized Denise had graduated two years ago. She and Ben were waiting to get married once he'd completed his Master's Degree.

I'm probably a good three years older than Rusty. . .is that going to matter, Lord?

"So how'd you and Mary Star meet? Does she go to Lakeview Bible too?"

"No. We met last year at my church's Christmas program. . ."

❧

Travis walked to the front entrance of his home, intending to lock up for the night. Through the screen door, he spied a blue van as it pulled to the front walkway. He waited around to see if he could guess the driver's objectives when, to his surprise, Jena jumped out of the passenger side. As the dim light illuminated the inside of the minivan, Travis strained to get a look at the driver. It was definitely a guy.

"Okay. See you tomorrow," he heard Jena say before slamming the door.

See you tomorrow? Travis raised a brow, wondering if Jena had forgotten her responsibilities included Saturdays. Or, what if she was planning to move out? Her male friend had a van. . .

Making his way through the house with purposeful strides, Travis exited the backdoor in time to meet Jena in the courtyard. She startled when she saw him, and Travis noticed the dark liquid that spilled from the cup in her hand, despite its white lid.

"Travis, you scared the wits out of me!"

He grinned. "Sorry." Cocking his head, he put his hands on

his hips. "Is that coffee?"

"Yeah."

"How can you sleep after drinking that stuff so late at night?"

"It's only ten o'clock."

"I'd be awake all night if I drank coffee at this hour."

Beneath the glow of the yard light, Travis watched as she shrugged out a reply.

"So, Jena," he began, slowing stepping toward her, "I, um, need to apologize for being so brusque earlier."

"That's okay. I knew you'd be mad."

"I'm not mad. Never was. Just, oh, maybe disappointed."

"Very understandable."

She took a few paces toward her apartment door, but Travis stepped in front of her.

"Jena, if you recall our initial agreement, I said you could have Sundays off."

"Right."

"Well. . ." Travis rubbed his palms together. "I didn't mean to eavesdrop, but I overheard you telling that guy in the van you'd see him tomorrow. Did you mean tomorrow night after eight?"

"No. I meant tomorrow during the day. We're going to the zoo, and I planned to take Mandi and Carly with me."

Travis didn't like the sound of it—Jena taking his daughters on a. . .date? No way!

"Look, Jena, I don't know. . ."

"Mary Star is coming and so is one of Rusty's friends."

"Rusty?"

"Yeah, the guy who drove me home tonight. He just graduated from Lakeview Bible, and he lives just across the street from you."

Travis pursed his lips and mulled over the remark. "What's his last name?"

"McKenna."

Travis recognized the name at once. Jill and Ryan McKenna were nice folks who had been a great help to Meg while she was sick. "I know the McKennas. So, you're interested in their son—what's his name? Rusty?"

"I don't know if I'm interested in him or not. I just met him tonight."

Travis folded his arms and regarded her sunburned face. She looked like Rudolph with that red nose. "Not to change the subject, but I think you got cooked at the beach today."

"I sure did. It's starting to smart now. I hope Mandi and Carly aren't sunburned. I doused them with sunscreen."

"And then there wasn't enough left for you, eh?"

"I thought there was. Guess not."

An uncomfortable little laugh escaped her, and she lowered her gaze. Travis, on the other hand, suddenly realized just what kind of woman Jena Calhoun was—a sacrificial one. She had made sure his daughters were spared sunburn even if it meant she got fried.

"Jena, you're a special lady, know that?"

She laughed again. "Uh-oh, sounds like you want another favor."

"Oh, thanks a heap," he retorted, sporting a grin. "I give you a compliment, and you think I'm just trying to butter you up."

"Well, you are a lawyer."

He brought his chin back, and she chuckled at his indignant expression. "I'll have you know I'm an honest lawyer."

She skirted around him and walked the rest of the way to her apartment's outer doorway. Her soft laughter wafted on the gentle breeze and seemed to wrap itself around his heart.

"I think you probably are an honest lawyer. You sure are a good daddy to your girls. They adore you."

"Thanks, but. . ." He frowned. "I don't get the connection."

"Well, maybe there isn't one—a logical one, anyway. It's just that, to my way of thinking, if you were a crooked, scheming attorney, it would probably come out somehow in your parenting."

"Hmm, interesting parallel." He couldn't help but think of Craig's son, Josh. At thirty years old, the man still behaved like a spoiled child, and it always made Travis cringe to hear the condescending tone Josh used whenever he talked to his wife.

"Good night, Travis."

Rousing himself from his musings, he saw Jena step inside the door. "Good night. Sleep well."

꙳

The next morning, much to Jena's dismay, she felt awful—so bad, in fact, that she phoned Star and cancelled their trip to the zoo. Telling Rusty when he came to pick her up at seven forty-five had been a major disappointment as well. But she felt so woozy and sick to her stomach that even the thought of traipsing around the zoo made her want to run for the bathroom. By noon, a drumbeat pounded in her head, and the sound of Travis mowing the lawn out in front of the house didn't help matters.

Sitting in the shady backyard, watching the girls splash in their kiddy pool, Jena held a cold rag to her temples.

"Miss Jena, what's the matter?" Mandi asked, climbing out of her pool and skipping to where Jena sat at the picnic table.

"Oh, nothing. I just have a little headache."

Mandi tipped her head while she contemplated the reply. "Aunty Glenda used to say me 'n Carly gave her a headache. Did we give you one too?"

"No, Precious. Neither of you gave it to me." Jena figured she probably just had a touch of the flu. She prayed she wouldn't pass the virus on to the girls.

Mandi returned to the pool, and minutes later, Travis rounded the corner of the yard. The girls shrieked with delight when he began splashing and tickling them. The racket made Jena tense.

"Hey, you still not feeling well?" Travis came over and sat down across from her. Beads of perspiration trickled down both sides of his face, getting lost somewhere in his shadowy jaw.

"No, I feel worse. I've got this headache that just won't quit."

"Did you take Ibuprofen or something?"

"Yes." She put the wet cloth across her eyes. It felt good. . . for a few seconds.

"Look at me, Jena."

Removing the cloth, she did as he bid her and glanced across the table at him. She suddenly felt like she'd gotten off one of those spinning rides at the fair.

"You look kind of punky." He tapered his brown eyes in a scrutinizing way. "You're going to the hospital."

"What?" Jena sat up a little straighter and watched him stand and leave the yard. Where was he going? "Travis, wait. . ."

She sighed when he didn't come back, thinking about her rotten health insurance. It only covered big things, like operations, and she couldn't afford a medical bill.

Carly climbed up into her lap. A look of concern pinched her three-year-old features. "How come Daddy said the hosible?"

"I don't know, Honey, but I'm going to be just fine." Jena couldn't help wondering if Travis was over-reacting because his wife had been so sick.

Within minutes, he returned with Mrs. Barlow in his wake. "I think she's got sunstroke or sun poisoning," he said.

A jab of fear caused Jena's heart to race—which only intensified the brain-twisting pain in her head.

"I'm happy to stay with the children, Travis," Mrs. Barlow said. She stroked Jena's hair back off her forehead. "Oh, you poor dear. You look like a lobster."

can ditch this place."

A tiny giggle escaped Jena's lips as she floated off to sleep again.

Grinning, Travis checked the score of the baseball game, then returned his attention to the magazine. He'd read two paragraphs into an article when the glass exam room door slid open, and Star entered, followed by a very tall young man with auburn hair.

"I got here as fast as I could," Star said. "Mrs. Barlow told me what happened. Is Jena going to be okay?"

Travis stood and put his forefinger to his lips. "She's sleeping," he whispered, "but, yes, she's going to be fine."

Star moved to Jena's bedside and stroked her hair. Seeing as he wouldn't get a formal introduction, Travis turned to the young man and stuck out his right hand. "Travis Larson."

"Oh, hi. . .Rusty McKenna."

They clasped hands, and Travis hoped his surprise didn't show on his face. *So this is Rusty.* Could Jena really be interested in this guy? In two sweeping glances, Travis decided Rusty stood about six-feet-five and had a mug that only a mother could love.

He cleared his throat. "I've, um, met your parents but haven't ever seen you around."

A goofy smile curved his lips. "That's probably 'cause I stayed in the dorms at school, even though the college is only about an hour's drive from here. Plus, during the past few summers I've been away on missions trips."

"Guess that explains it." Travis forced a polite smile, digesting the information. He told himself he shouldn't be shocked that Jena was interested in a man who shared her religious beliefs. But at the same time, it irked him. Then, it bothered him that he felt irked.

He glanced at Jena only to see her sitting up in bed.

"What do you think you're doing?" he asked, walking to the side of the hospital bed. Placing his hand on her shoulder, he gently pushed her back against the pillow. Her curly strawberry-blond hair splayed against the puffy white surface, and in that moment, Jena reminded him of Sleeping Beauty in one of his daughters' fairy-tale books.

"Travis, I feel better. I want to go home."

Leaning against the guardrails, he gazed down at her, feeling oddly mesmerized.

"Travis. . .did you hear me?"

"What? Oh, yeah. . .I heard you." He forced himself to focus on the situation at hand "Listen, you'll go home when the doctors say you can go home. Which reminds me. . ." He looked over at Star. "Can you spend the night with her? I don't think Jena should be alone up in her apartment tonight."

"Sure. I'll call my parents and let them know." Star glanced down at Jena. "We'll take care of you, Honey. You just peep, and we'll be there for you."

"Oh, good grief."

Travis smirked. "Too bad you're so sunburned, Jena. Now we can't see you blush."

With an exasperated moan, she pulled the sheet up over her face, and Travis laughed.

❧

"Are you sure you're okay, Jena? I mean, maybe I should have Travis come up here and take your temperature or something."

"Shut up!" Jena laughed and threw a pillow at Star.

It smacked her shoulder, and Star chuckled. "Well, he's only phoned twice in the past hour-and-a-half to make sure you're all right."

Jena sighed. "Yeah, but that's because Bella Minniati can't take 'no' for an answer. Travis tried to get out of going to church tomorrow morning and lunch afterwards, but Bella won't hear of it. She told him that if I'm too sick, he has to come and bring the girls. Of course, Travis won't argue because he still hopes Bella will sign on with his law firm."

"Oh what a tangled web we weave. . ."

"Amen!"

Sitting on the opposite end of the couch, Star whipped the pillow back at her, but Jena caught it easily. "So what do you think of Rusty?"

The smile slipped from Star's heart-shaped face. "Do you like him, Jena? I mean. . .romantically speaking?"

At Star's tone, Jena's guard went up. "Why do you ask?"

"Well, because. . .I'm rather attracted to him for some odd reason. He's really not my type at all. I always imagined myself marrying a guy like Travis Larson."

Disappointment swelled in Jena's chest. "What about Tom? You've been dating him on and off for some time now."

"Yeah, well, we're off again. He's got some weird phobia about commitments. But then along comes Rusty. . .and this afternoon he said he'd been asking God if he could meet me, so when he ran into you last night, it was like the Lord answered his prayer." Star shrugged and two rosy spots suddenly appeared on her cheeks. "I guess I thought that was really romantic. Rusty obviously doesn't have a problem with the idea of lasting relationships."

"That's awesome," Jena replied, even though she felt like sobbing. Rusty had been drawn to Star the entire time, and now Jena felt stupid for thinking it was she who'd sparked his interest. "Well, listen, I'm going to bed. Are you sure you'll be okay here on the sofa?"

"I'm totally fine. I'm just going to read a chapter in my Bible and go to sleep."

"Okay. G'night." Jena walked to her bedroom. Inside, she

closed the door and leaned against it as the first of many tears trickled from her eyes.

ॐ

The next morning, the sunshine streamed in through her bedroom window and woke Jena. It was like a hug and smile from her Heavenly Father. Her disappointment had ebbed, and Jena felt more determined than ever to trust God with her future. So what if she ended up husbandless? There were worse fates in life. Jena decided that if she never married, she would simply be a blessing to another family.

After showering, she donned the best outfit she owned, a navy blue coatdress that had white buttons down the front and bold white trim along its V-neck. Her tight, sunburned skin protested her every move, but Jena ignored it. If she ended up a missionary in a third-world country, there would be no concessions for a pampered little rose. She'd have to be as strong as a willow in order to weather the climate and rough conditions. She might as well start now.

Feeling determined, Jena headed over to Travis's where she prepared a light breakfast. After Mandi and Carly woke up, she gathered their clothes and led them downstairs into the sunny den where she helped the two little ones into frilly summertime dresses that looked as though they'd never been worn. By the time Travis entered the kitchen, Jena had finished arranging both girls' hair and now encouraged them to eat their cereal and toast.

"Daddy, don't we look pretty!" Mandi exclaimed. She jumped off her chair and twirled around on one heel of her shiny black Mary Jane's.

He nodded distractedly and looked at Jena. "You're supposed to be in bed recuperating."

"I'm recuperated."

"No." Travis shook his head. "The doctor made it clear

you're to rest for at least forty-eight hours. Now scoot."

Jena knew he was right, but she didn't think going to church would put that much of a strain on her body. "I can rest this afternoon. I'm not a docile little thing. I'm an able-bodied woman."

"Yeah, and I aim to keep you that way so I won't have to miss work tomorrow." He inclined his head toward the back door.

"Travis, I—"

"Don't argue with me, Jena."

His tone and stern expression left no room for debate, although she glimpsed a compassionate light in his cocoa brown eyes as he finished knotting his tie.

Returning a small smile, she stood and pushed in the kitchen chair under the table. "All right, you win," she said, making her way to the back door.

"Thanks for dressing the girls and fixing their hair," he called after her. "I appreciate it."

She glanced at him from over her shoulder. "You're welcome."

"And get some rest, you hear?"

Unable to help herself, Jena saluted.

He narrowed his gaze at her as if warning her not to be so sassy, and she chuckled all the way back to her apartment. Entering the living room, she heard Star singing in the shower. She, too, would be leaving for church soon. Jena glanced around her apartment and wondered what she'd do with her time. She was accustomed to staying busy, barely having a moment to think, let alone hours of idleness.

She walked into her bedroom where she undressed and hung up her good clothes. She slipped off her stockings, stuffing them in her top dresser drawer. Next, she pulled on a yellow printed cotton skirt with a loose elastic waistline and a matching yellow t-shirt. The material felt so soft against her damaged skin that a small sigh of relief escaped Jena's lips.

Perhaps Travis had been right in ordering her to rest. She wasn't quite up to par yet.

An hour later, after Star left, Jena pulled out her Bible and proceeded to have some personal devotion time. She praised God for all her blessings, including her summer job. Sunburn aside, the first week had gone extremely well, and at the hospital, the admitting registrar had taken a charity application designed for those, like Jena, who didn't have quality health insurance. Jena asked forgiveness for envying Star and Rusty and prayed the Lord to lead in that relationship. She continued to pray, pleading with God to help her feel complacent as a single woman and to use her to further His heavenly kingdom.

It was then that Jena felt a special burden for Travis's soul. *Oh, please, dear Lord Jesus, let him hear the Good News loud and clear this morning. Open his heart so he understands why You left Your Ivory Palace to live as a Man of little means and die a cruel death for our sins. I also pray for Mandi and Carly. Whet their appetite for Your word and. . .help them behave. . .*

After finishing her petition, the heaviness in her spirit for Travis didn't abate. She prayed again. Then once more. At long last, she gave the matter over to God, trusting that the outcome would be to His glory.

fifteen

Travis tried to stifle another yawn as he sat to Joe Minniati's left. He forced a complacent expression while he listened to the pastor drone on about some such thing. Glancing at Joe who appeared attentive, occasionally scribbling down a few notes, Travis decided he'd best pay attention in case the Minnatis wanted to discuss the message over lunch.

"The Bible was written as proof and testimony of the deity of Jesus Christ," said the bald-headed, African-American man at the pulpit. He had a kind-sounding voice despite the austere look on his face. "There is no way anyone can dispute the fact that Jesus Christ is God, sent from God, and is the second Person of the Trinity after reading this Book."

Travis glanced at the Bible in his lap. It had belonged to Meg, and the passage in Colossians from which the pastor's message had been derived was underlined with a purple fine-point pen. Meg had believed this book. She'd been a devoted Christian.

"And why anyone wouldn't come to Christ after reading John chapter three and 'You must be born again' is a mystery to me," the pastor continued. "If Jesus said it, we'd better do it."

That phrase—"come to Christ"—triggered the memory of a promise Travis had made to Meg on her deathbed. Her last wish was that he would "come to Christ" so she would see him in Heaven, and Travis vowed he would. Then, again, he would have lassoed the moon for Meg at that point just to ease her burden. He'd felt so helpless, watching her die.

"Come to Christ"—what did that mean? How did a person

go about "coming to Christ"? Was there a ritual involved? Did he have to join a church? Travis tried to remember how Meg "came to Christ," but he couldn't recall. He thought she might have had some sort of religious experience shortly after Mandi was born, but he didn't know what brought it about.

Sorry, Meg, I just don't understand.

The congregation suddenly stood to its feet, and Travis realized the sermon had ended. After a short prayer, the pianist began to plunk out a lively melody, and church members vacated their pews and filled the aisles, laughing, talking, and greeting each other.

"What did you think, Travis?" Bella asked. She'd been sitting on the other side of her husband.

"Your pastor is very articulate," he replied lamely.

"He's an educated man," Joe said. "He's got an earned doctorate. He served in the Air Force and has his pilot's license, so he's big on mission aviation."

"What's 'mission aviation?' " Travis couldn't help asking as they left the sanctuary.

"Pastor Richards has flown to third-world countries," Bella answered, "to feed starving people who need the Bread of Life."

"Hmm, I see." Standing in the foyer, he glanced to his left. "This way to pick up my girls?"

Bella shook her head. "No, this way." She motioned to the right. "I hope they had a good time. They're adorable, Travis. I'm just sorry Jena couldn't come today. She's an absolute doll. . . and she fixed the girls' hair so cute."

Travis expelled a long breath and followed a babbling Bella down a crowded corridor and into a large room where the pastor's wife held what the Minniatis called "Children's Church." Inside, Mandi and Carly were having so much fun playing with the toys and the other children that it took Travis a few minutes to get their attention. Once they spotted him, however, they dropped what they were doing and came running, their arms outstretched. The sight warmed Travis's heart.

❧

Jena sat in the shady courtyard, relaxing on the chaise lounge and reading a collection of stories about women who became brides on the Oregon Trail. She enjoyed adventurous wholesome romances, particularly about brides-to-be. Jena prayed she would get married someday, but she figured it didn't hurt to read about the thrills and frills surrounding weddings, and she couldn't recall when she'd last been able to enjoy some good fiction. Attending college and working several odd jobs that accommodated her schedule didn't leave much room for relaxation. But her minor debilitation proved to be something of a blessing. Jena had even found time to phone her parents this morning. Of course, the conversations with her mother, father, and brother never got past superficial topics as they each told her about their busy lives. No one asked about Jena and that hurt. It seemed as if her family couldn't see beyond themselves—but that wasn't new, and she told herself she shouldn't feel surprised. She'd just have to pray harder.

"Hello, Dearie. . ."

Glancing up, Jena watched Mrs. Barlow enter the small yard. Dressed in a blue and white dress, it appeared the older woman had just come back from church. "What are you doing home? I thought your Sunday afternoons were reserved for your grandchildren."

Smiling, Mrs. Barlow took a seat in a nearby lawn chair. "I was worried about you, so after having lunch with my son and his family, I thought I'd drive back and make sure you're all right."

"I'm fine." Jena felt a tad guilty for worrying her sweet friend.

"Is Travis home? Things sound too quiet around here. Are Mandi and Carly gone?"

"No. . .and yes," Jena replied with a little laugh at the "too quiet" remark. "Nobody's home. Travis took the girls to church with him. He was invited by the Minniatis."

"You don't say? Why, Meg would be ecstatic to hear he took his daughters to hear the preaching of The Word. She tried and tried to get Travis to attend with her. He always said he was too busy."

Jena's heart constricted. "What a shame." She wondered if he regretted those "I'm too busy" decisions now.

The sound of a car pulling into the driveway drew Jena's attention, and she looked up in time to see the front quarter panel of Travis's shining black Lexus. Within no time at all, Mandi skipped into the courtyard.

"Well, hello, Darling!" Mrs. Barlow said with a broad grin.

"Hi!" Mandi sat down on the edge of Jena's chair.

Jena smiled. "Did you have fun at church today?"

"Uh-huh. We sang and drew pictures, then Mrs. Smith told us a story about a boy named David who killed a mean giant."

Jena's smile grew just as Travis entered the yard, carrying a sleeping Carly over his shoulder.

"I hope you've been resting," he told Jena before greeting Mrs. Barlow.

"I have, so don't worry. How'd it go this morning?"

"Fine." Travis grinned. "I think Bella's going to sign."

"That's great news!"

"Sure is." Reaching the back door, Travis pulled the keys from his pocket. "Come on, Mandi. Nap time."

"But I'm not tired," she whined.

Travis narrowed his gaze, giving his daughter that sardonic lawyer look for which Jena found him so famous. She bit back a laugh, thinking he might be able to intimidate jurors, but poor Travis had little influence on Mandi.

"I'm too big for a nap, Daddy." The girl turned to Jena, her childish brown eyes pleading for an ally. "Right?"

"Obey your father," Jena prompted on an encouraging note.

Pouting, Mandi rose from the lawn chair and stomped to the backdoor. Mrs. Barlow put her fingers over her lips in an effort to hide her amusement.

"If I'm not too old for a nap, neither are you," Travis said, following his oldest daughter into the house.

The screen door squeaked on its hinges, closing behind the Larson family.

Jena chuckled at Travis' parting remark and glanced at Mrs. Barlow.

"Travis is such a good father, isn't he?"

"Yes, he is." Jena didn't have to think twice before answering. "Now, tell me what I missed at church this morning. Did Star have a guest?"

"Why, yes. Rusty McKenna, our neighbor right across the street. Do you know him?"

"Just met him." Disappointment gave her a hard jab, but it felt more annoying than painful. "I'm praying for them."

"Well, I was surprised to say the least. I would have never thought Rusty and Star. . ."

Mrs. Barlow giggled like a girl, causing Jena to laugh too.

They continued chatting for quite some time before Jena heard the backdoor open. Glancing off to her right, she half-expected to see Mandi, sneaking outside and abandoning her naptime. But instead, she saw Travis striding toward them. He'd changed from his suit and tie and now wore blue jeans and a short-sleeved T-shirt.

"Hey, can I ask you two something?" Reaching the adjacent lawn chair, he sat down.

"Sure."

"Yes, of course, Travis," Mrs. Barlow reiterated. "What is it?"

Leaning forward, he studied his hands dangling over his knees before meeting Jena's gaze. "What does 'come to Christ' mean?"

Taken by surprised, she blinked. "Isn't the phrase self-explanatory?"

"Not to me. My family attended a myriad of churches when I was growing up and only on special occasions. But my wife had beliefs similar to yours." He glanced across the way. "And yours too, Mrs. Barlow—and the Minniatis' too. Before she died, Meg said she wanted me to 'come to Christ.' But I just don't know how."

Jena noted the earnest expression on his face and the beseeching look in his dark eyes. Her heart melted with compassion. *Oh, Lord, Travis is like that prisoner in the Book of Acts who asked, "What must I do to be saved?" Give Mrs. Barlow and me the right words to answer him.*

"Well, Travis, 'coming to Christ' refers to one's salvation experience," the older woman began, "and no two conversions are alike. For instance, I was a young girl when I became a Christian. Jena, what about you?"

"I came to Christ one night when I was in high school. I visited a friend's youth group, and after hearing the pastor's message, I realized I was a sinner and had no hope of eternal life, except by believing in Jesus Christ as the only Way to heaven. Jesus is God and Man. He lived a perfect life here on earth and allowed Roman soldiers to crucify Him so that—"

She paused, seeing Travis's confused expression. "Maybe we could explain better if we showed you some verses in the Bible."

"Good idea," said Mrs. Barlow with an approving nod of her head.

Jena swung her legs off the lawn chair and stood. "I'll go get mine. It's upstairs."

"I've got Meg's Bible in the kitchen. Want to use that one?"

"Um, sure." *Oh, Lord, he's so open!*

Excitement coursed through Jena as she followed Mrs. Barlow and Travis into the house. But she tried to keep a level head as they took seats at the kitchen table.

Jena watched as Mrs. Barlow reverently opened Meg's Bible to the Book of Romans. She noticed verse twenty-three in chapter three had been underlined.

"Look, Travis," Mrs. Barlow said, "God's Word tells us that all have sinned and come short of the glory of God. None of us is perfect. We've all done things wrong. Do you agree with that?"

"Sure."

"Okay, then. . ." The kindly neighbor lady flipped to the twenty-third verse of chapter six. It too had been underlined with blue ink. "God says, 'For the wages of sin is death. . .' See, because we've done wrong, there are consequences. Just like when your daughters act up. You have to discipline them. Because we've sinned, we deserve eternal punishment since God cannot allow sin into heaven. But look what the latter part of this passage says, 'but the gift of God is eternal life through Jesus Christ our Lord.'"

Jena sent up prayer after prayer, while Mrs. Barlow paged back to the Book of John and found the sixteenth verse in chapter three. It had been highlighted in yellow marker. *For God so loved the world, that he gave his only begotten Son, that whosoever believeth in him should not perish, but have everlasting life.*

"God gave us His Son, Jesus Christ, to take our punishment," Mrs. Barlow explained. "Our Heavenly Father sacrificed for us, just like you would sacrifice for Mandi and Carly."

Pursing his lips and looking thoughtful, Travis nodded.

Mrs. Barlow returned to the Book of Romans and found

chapter five, verse eight. It, like the others, had been underlined. "But God commanded his love toward us in that, while we were yet sinners, Christ died for us." She glanced up from the Bible. "Travis, do you understand about sin and its consequences?"

"Yep. That's one thing I do understand." He sat back in his chair. "The courts prosecute sinners everyday. When people break the law, they have to pay the price."

"Exactly." Mrs. Barlow smiled, and Jena felt elated that the truth of the gospel was getting through to him. "But in this case, Jesus stepped up and told the Judge that he would pay for our crimes. He died on the cross for us. But on the third day, God raised Him from the dead. Jesus is alive today—and those who believe will live forever with Him."

"Except we have to die first. . ." Travis interjected.

Jena noted the faraway look in his eyes. She sensed Travis was thinking of his deceased wife. "That's the sin-cursed part of this life," she said. "It'll end in death. The cold, hard fact is everybody is going to die sometime. But where we'll spend our eternity is the decision we make while we're living."

"That's right. Here, look. . ." Mrs. Barlow turned to Romans chapter ten verse nine. "And this is how a person 'comes to Christ,' Travis." She showed him the verse. *That if thou shalt confess with thy mouth the Lord Jesus, and shalt believe in thine heart that God hath raised him from the dead, thou shalt be saved.*

"Do you believe that, Travis?"

A pensive expression crossed his face as his soul hung in the balance. Jena prayed as hard as she knew how. *Please, God, let him understand all this. . .*

"You know what?" he answered at last, "I do believe it. I'll tell you why. I saw something different in my wife after she 'came to Christ' when Mandi was a baby. Over the years, I watched Meg devote herself to our daughter and me. She was so different from my friends' wives. I felt like the luckiest guy on earth. Meg didn't care about material things or push me up the corporate ladder or flirt at dinner parties. When she found out she was pregnant again, she put Carly's life before her own after she learned she had cancer." Travis drew in a deep breath then shook his head. "Scores of people advised Meg to terminate her pregnancy so she could get chemotherapy, but she refused—for Carly's sake."

Tears sprang into Jena's eyes, and she pressed her lips together in an effort to stave off her emotion.

Travis tapped a finger on the open Bible. "And I believe this is true, Mrs. Barlow, because I've seen it in you over the years. . . and now I've seen it Jena too." He looked across the table at her and their gazes met. "For a single lady, you're really different—and I mean that as a compliment. After one week, I've seen how hard you work, the kind way in which you take care of my girls. You don't swear or watch smut on TV, and you don't have men coming and going all hours of the day and night." He paused, his dark gaze penetrating hers. "I know there's a God in heaven, Jena, because you brought Him back into my house."

She swatted at her tears. "Oh, Travis, I've got plenty of faults. But I'm so blessed to hear that you've seen Jesus in me."

"I have. Know what else? I think Meg would really like you."

Jena could barely find her voice. "I think I would have liked Meg too."

"She was a lovely person," Mrs. Barlow stated wistfully. But then her age-lined face broke into a grin. "But it was definitely no accident that Jena came to work for you, Travis. Somehow I knew she was the one for the summer girl job."

"You were right."

He chuckled and sent Jena a wink that made her cheeks

flame with embarrassment. *Good thing I'm already pink from my sunburn.*

"Well, young man, you have a decision to make."

"I do?" He glanced at Mrs. Barlow with questions pooling in his eyes.

"Do you want to get saved?" she asked in a caring tone. "Do you want to 'come to Christ?'"

"Umm. . .that depends. What do I have to do? Walk over hot coals or something?"

Jena couldn't suppress the laugh that bubbled up inside her.

"No, Silly," Mrs. Barlow said with a smile. "Here, look." She pointed to verse thirteen and read, "'For whosoever shall call upon the name of the Lord shall be saved.' You just pray, Travis. Confess your sins to Christ, ask for forgiveness, then ask Him to save you. You come to Christ in prayer."

"That's it?" He brought his chin back in surprise.

"That's it."

"Okay. . ." But suddenly he looked so lost. "Uh, praying is sort of unfamiliar territory for me."

"Would you like Jena and me to pray with you?"

He nodded out a silent reply.

Jena gave him a smile and stretched her arm across the table, offering him her hand. Travis took it, then clasped Mrs. Barlow's hand as well.

"Just repeat after me, all right?"

"All right."

Trying to squelch her anticipation, Jena forced herself to concentrate as Mrs. Barlow led Travis in prayer.

"Dear God, I confess to You my sinfulness. . ." She paused to let Travis echo her. "I'm sorry for all the wrong things I've said and done, and I understand that it was because of me and my sin that Jesus went to the cross and died. . .I ask You to forgive me, and I ask Jesus to come into my heart and live forever. . .I ask You to save me. . .Thank You for this most precious gift of eternal life that I now accept. . .In Jesus' name, Amen."

When Travis finished, Jena lifted her gaze and searched his face. "Did you mean it?"

"Every word."

"Well, then. . ." She squeezed his hand and smiled. "You came to Christ and were saved."

"Congratulations, Travis," Mrs. Barlow said as tears of joy filled her rheumy eyes. "The angels are now rejoicing in heaven!"

sixteen

The following morning, Jena helped the girls dress, then after baking a pan of brownies, she took them to her church's Memorial Day picnic. The sky was overcast in the beginning, but the humidity thickened once the sun appeared. While Jena expected to have a fun time at the outing, despite the clammy weather, everything that could go wrong did. Mandi whined and complained because she wanted pizza for lunch, not a grilled hamburger. Next, she thoughtlessly tossed a ball in the air and it landed on another little girl's head, bringing an aggravated father to the picnic table at which Jena was sitting. Carly wet her pants, and Jena had forgotten to pack extra clothes, so she gathered up their things and walked the girls to the car. . .only to realize she'd locked the keys inside the Volvo. Three men tried to open the hatch but were unsuccessful, so Jena had to use Star's cell phone and call Travis, who had planned to take the day to catch up on some paperwork. From the tone of his voice, Jena could tell that he was not thrilled to be summoned across town to a picnic because his summer girl had left her brain at home that morning.

"So much for my glowing attributes," Jena said, handing the phone back to Star.

"You're human. So what? Besides, this is probably some satanic attack because you led Travis to Christ. You rocked the Evil One's kingdom, so he's striking back." She grinned. "But you're on the winning side, and Travis is a Christian now. How cool is that?"

"Very cool." Jena smiled, marveling at her friend's perception.

Star was a relatively new Christian too. "But salvation is only the beginning. How do I get Travis interested in a Bible study?"

"That's God's department."

"Right." Jena felt properly chastened.

At that moment, Tammy Bissell approached them. A heavyset, well-intentioned woman, Tammy offered Jena the use of her daughter's spare outfit so Carly could get out of her wet things.

"You're a godsend, Mrs. Bissell. Thanks." Leaving Mandi under Star's supervision, Jena took Carly to the rustic, park restrooms where she washed and changed the little girl. But Carly didn't like the shorts set and pitched a fit. Jena felt her nerves begin to fray.

Deciding there was no point in arguing with the three-year-old, Jena put the wet clothes back on, only to have Carly change her mind and want to wear the other outfit after all. On the way back to the car, Jena felt like a hypocrite. She'd been tempted to throttle Carly in the bathroom for having a hissy fit, and yet she'd given Travis the impression that she was great with kids. Guess she wasn't so great with them after all. Did that mean she'd selected the wrong major in college? Jena sighed. Maybe she wasn't cut out to manage a daycare center, which meant the last eight years of her life had been a complete waste of time.

Or maybe I'm still in the stages of recuperation. An instant later, she realized that was exactly her problem. After all, she'd had sun poisoning this weekend. Anyone would feel less than patient and loving under those conditions. *Thank You, Father, for helping me understand myself.*

Up ahead in the parking lot, Jena saw that Travis had arrived. Star, Rusty, and Mandi stood nearby while he opened the Volvo wagon's hatch and retrieved the car keys.

"Sorry to have inconvenienced you," Jena said to Travis

when she reached him.

He tossed the keys at her, accompanied by a long look. But whether it stemmed from exasperation or amusement, Jena couldn't tell.

"Travis Larson! What in the world are you doing here?"

The deep voice of Derek Ryan drew Jena's gaze. A man of medium height and build, she didn't know him well, but suddenly she remembered what little she did know about him: Mr. Ryan was an attorney. Like Travis!

"Hey, Man, good to see you again." Travis stuck out his right hand, and Derek clasped it before balling his other fist and giving Travis a friendly sock in the arm.

"I didn't know you were here at the picnic."

"I'm not. My summer girl needed my, um, assistance." Travis glanced Jena's way and cleared his throat loudly. She shrugged, but in that moment, she knew Travis wasn't miffed at her.

"Your. . .who? Summer girl?" A blank expression crossed Derek's face.

"I work for Travis, taking care of his daughters," Jena explained. "For the summer."

"Oh, I get it." He grinned. Raking a hand through his light brown hair, he turned back to Travis. "You up for a ballgame?"

"Naw, I've got tons of work to do."

"Okay." A goading gleam brightened Ryan's eyes. "You're probably too out of shape anyway, you old man."

"Yeah, right. I'm no older than you are, and I could take you on in sports any day—just like I do in the courtroom."

Oh, brother! In Jena's opinion, guys were all ego and appetite—and out of the two, they were mostly ego.

"Prove it, Larson. Join our game this afternoon. Let's see what you're made of."

Travis stared off in the distance; his eyes narrowed and

seemed to weigh the options. He glanced at Jena, and she decided to get out of the line of scrimmage by walking over to where Star and Rusty stood. Mandi had left for the swings and seemed to be getting along with the other kids. A teenage girl pushed them one at a time, higher, higher, causing the children to squeal with delight.

Folding her arms, Jena returned her attention to Travis who had tossed Carly over his shoulder like a sack of potatoes.

"You're on, Derek."

"Great. We play with a softball, so you outta be able to get a few hits in."

With one hand on Carly, Travis chuckled and pointed a warning forefinger at his challenger. "Just keep that pretty head of yours low."

Derek laughed. "C'mon. Follow me to yonder baseball field."

❧

Two days later, Travis sat in his office at Duncan, Duncan, and Larson and massaged his right arm. He must have been nuts to think he could play softball without warming up. What did he think, that he was still seventeen? The only consolation was that Derek admitted to being just as sore. They had shared a good laugh over it before court this morning.

"Travis?"

Looking up, he saw Marci, his firm's secretary, standing in the doorway. A dark haired woman in her fifties, Marci had a nervous demeanor, and she flitted around the office like a crazed hummingbird.

"Bella Minniati is here to see you."

"Great. Send her in."

Travis cleared off his desk in time to greet Bella as she entered his office and closed the door.

"Travis, how are you?"

"Terrific. How 'bout yourself?"

"I still get morning sickness, but at least the nausea doesn't linger throughout the day anymore."

Nodding, he offered Bella one of the maroon leather chairs in front of his desk. "Meg was sick a lot at first too."

Bella replied with an empathetic grin. "I've got the contract here." She reached into her briefcase and pulled out the document. "I rewrote a section before signing it. Here. Take a look."

Travis read it through, noting it stated that he was to act as the exclusive attorney for the Milwaukee Mavericks team. If he ever left Duncan, Duncan, and Larson, the team would remain his client and could not be handed off to either of his partners.

"Craig'll never go for this," Travis said, tossing the contract onto his desk.

"Then I don't sign." Bella sat forward. "Personally, Trav, I think you should get rid of Duncan and Duncan. I don't trust Craig, and I've heard from a reputable source that his son is a chip off the ol' block."

"Look, Bella, that topic isn't open for discussion. I'll have Craig read over the contract, but I can guarantee he won't approve it."

She sat back, and her eyes sparked with something akin to mischief. "Come to work for the Mavericks. The team has enough issues to keep any lawyer busy, and we'll pay you a handsome salary."

Travis chewed the corner of his lip in contemplation. "Hmm. . .it's tempting."

"Think about it."

"I will."

Their meeting lasted a while longer, then Travis escorted Bella into the lobby.

"Tell Jena hello for me."

"Will do."

Bella paused before exiting the firm's office suites. "You know, Travis, I really should give you fair warning. I plan to steal your summer girl. Joe and I are mulling over the idea of purchasing a daycare center. There are big bucks in daycare these days, and Jena would make an awesome director. I have no doubt that she'd hire the most competent staff." Bella gave her abdomen a loving pat. "And I'm going to need responsible, caring people to watch Junior. . ."

Travis did his best to act nonchalant. "Jena's a free agent."

"So she is." Bella's red lips curved into a broad smile. "Tah-tah for now, Travis. Get back to me soon about that contract."

He nodded and watched the impeccably dressed woman sashay to the elevators. Then, turning, he made his way back to his office deciding that Bella Minniati would steal his summer girl over his dead body. Lifting the telephone, Travis called home.

❧

"Hi, Jen, how're things?"

"Fine." Sitting in the yard, holding the cordless phone, Jena smiled. "Mandi and Carly are watering the flowers we planted. It's so cute the way they carry around their toy watering cans."

A chuckle came forth from the other end of the line. "You're staying out of the sun, I hope."

"Yes. . ."

"Say, listen. I've been thinking. You're working out great, the girls adore you—

"I adore them too." Jena meant every word. Sure, Mandi had her whiny moments and Carly had her three-year-old meltdowns, but Jena was rapidly learning how to deal with both girls without feeling frazzled.

"I can tell you're fond of my daughters. That's why I wondered if you would consider staying on in the fall."

"No, I can't. I have one semester left of school, and I've worked too hard and too long not to finish my degree."

"I understand. I'm not asking you to drop out of college. We'll work around your classes."

"That might be difficult since I attend a school that's more than an hour away."

"You'll have a car and a rent-free apartment. Won't those two perks make up for the long commute?"

"Hmm. Maybe."

Jena heard Travis's deep laugh. "I'll draw up a contract and bring it home tonight."

She frowned. "Contract? We don't need a contract."

"Oh, yes we do. With people like Bella Minniati in the world, we need a contract."

"Bella? What's she got to do with my working for you?"

A pause. "Nothing." Travis's tone turned somber. "I'll see you tonight."

"Okay." Jena felt totally confused. . .and a bit worried. "Travis, did I do something wrong?"

"Not at all. You're the best, Jen."

She rolled her eyes.

"By the way, what are you making for supper?"

"Anything you want," she quipped, figuring she would appeal to the appetite side of him, and maybe he'd snap out of whatever funk he'd gotten into. "Name it."

"I'm not picky," Travis replied. "Just don't make anything. . . Italian."

She frowned. Didn't he like Italian food? "All right. . ."

"See you later."

"Bye." Jena pushed the OFF button on the phone and decided that was the weirdest call she'd had in all of her born days.

seventeen

True to his word, Travis had a contract drawn up, and Jena signed it. The terms were obvious. For the next twelve months, she agreed to take care of Mandi and Carly and, in return, he promised to allow her to finish college, pay her the same salary she presently earned, along with providing her room and board and unlimited use of his car. What a deal! How could she go wrong? But Jena knew she would eventually have to begin a career. Working for Travis, however, would enable her to finish school and save some money in the process. Then, during the last few months of her employment, she could do some job hunting. By this time next year, Jena hoped to be working in her field of expertise.

"Are you from around here?" Travis asked as he folded his copy of their signed contract. "I don't recall you mentioning your family."

"No, I'm from California."

"Really?" Travis sat back in his handsome leather desk chair. "You're a long way from home, little girl."

"I'm not so little. I'll be twenty-seven at the end of August."

Travis grinned at her tart reply. "I talk to my parents almost every day, and Meg's folks call from Minnesota at least once a week."

"Consider yourself blessed, Travis. My family isn't close. We never have been. Each of us has always operated independently. I talk to my parents once a month—if I can catch them at home—and I've only gone back to California once since I started college. Wisconsin is my home now."

"That's too bad—about your family, I mean."

"Yes, but I can't change them. I can only determine to do things differently when I get married and have kids."

"When?" Travis lifted one dark brow. "Is there something I should know?"

Jena laughed. "I just signed a one-year contract to work for you. What do you think?"

"Just checking." He smirked and sat forward. Pursing his lips, he regarded her in a thoughtful manner. "Hey, I'm curious. . .and I mean no offense by this, but it seems to be taking you an unusually long time to finish college. Did you change your major a couple of times?"

"No. I just didn't want to take out any loans." Jena had become accustomed to people questioning her lengthy college stint. Where once she felt embarrassed about it, she now held her head up with dignity. "I've paid my entire way through school, with the exception of grant and scholarship money. God provided me with the job opportunities and the classes to fit my budget each semester."

"Quite commendable."

"I think so. I read somewhere that the average grad ends his college career more than thirty thousand dollars in debt. I decided long ago that if I ever married a man in the ministry, I wouldn't want to burden him financially with my school loans. So I made up my mind to pay my own way."

"I'm impressed, Jena." Travis tipped his head. "A man in the ministry. . .is that what you're looking for in a husband? You want a guy like Rusty?"

Jena lowered her gaze and deliberately skirted his question. For some odd reason, she didn't want to discuss boyfriends—or lack thereof—with Travis. "Rusty is interested in Star."

"Yeah, I kind of wondered after seeing them together yesterday. Are you upset?"

"Not at all." She meant that too. Sure, she had been disappointed at first. But she'd soon gotten over it. Now she felt happy for her friends.

Jena glanced at her wristwatch and realized Star would be knocking at her door any minute. Tuesday nights were reserved for their discipleship lesson, although last week they hadn't met because Jena was still settling into her apartment and adjusting to her new job.

She stood. "I should get going. Star's coming over tonight."

"All right." Travis stood also. "I'll see you in the morning."

"Good night."

His expression couldn't be easily defined, although a soft light appeared in his brown eyes. "Night, Jena."

❧

As the week advanced, Travis found himself easing into a comfortable routine. The girls were happy, and Jena proved to be a master at organization. She even clipped coupons before grocery shopping. The cupboards were stocked, the refrigerator full, and each bathroom had a convenient supply of toilet paper beneath its vanity. Oddly, those common necessities often fueled veritable crises while his sister Glenda was in charge. But since he no longer had to fret about his home situation, Travis put more effort into his career. He won a long-shot lawsuit, and with that victory, came the praise of his colleague, Craig Duncan.

"Trav, I think you're back to your old self. I'll admit I was worried for a while."

Placing his attaché case on his desk, Travis glanced over his shoulder and grinned at the older man. "I was worried for a while too. But now that I have a summer girl. . ."

"Oh, yes, Susie Homemaker herself."

"Hey, don't knock it."

"I won't, I won't. If it works for you, great." Clearing his throat, Craig took a seat in a nearby armchair. "Now, correct me if I'm wrong, but did I hear you talking to someone on the phone about attending a. . .a Bible study?"

"You're a seasoned eavesdropper." Travis laughed. "But, yes, to answer your question. Derek Ryan leads the study once a week in his home."

"Derek Ryan. . .do I know him?"

"Yep, he works for Liberty International."

"Oh, that's right. He's one of those guys obsessed with religious freedoms."

"Somebody's got to do it."

"I suppose." Craig yawned.

Travis placed his hands on his hips. "Not to change the subject, but did you read the contract Bella dropped off last week?"

Craig snapped his fingers. "Yes, and I signed both copies. So did Josh. I'll go get the paperwork. I meant to give it to you yesterday."

He signed it? Travis felt himself gape as he watched his business partner stride to his own office and return with the contract.

"Here you go." He tossed the papers onto Travis's briefcase.

"And you, um, read the whole thing?"

"Sure. If Bella wants you to act exclusively on the behalf of the Mavericks, that's fine by me."

Travis rubbed his jaw. Craig had obviously stopped there and didn't read the rest of the contract's terms. "You want to read it over once more—just to be sure everything's in order?"

"What for? Now, look, Travis. I might be pushing sixty-five, but I've got my wits about me. Do you doubt that?"

"Nope."

"Well, okay then. Give Bella her copy. . .and I'm glad it's you who has to deal with that woman and not me. How 'bout we celebrate your recent successes by stopping at The Black Tie and having a few drinks before going home?"

Travis shrugged. "Okay. Sure."

"Great. I'll let Josh and Yolanda know. . .and maybe Marci will even want to tag along." Smiling, Craig walked out of the office.

Travis lowered himself into his chair and loosened his tie. He felt more concerned than ever about his affiliation with Duncan and Duncan. It bothered him that Craig skimmed through the Mavericks' contract. Craig's lackadaisical attitude could cost the firm everything.

So what do I do now? Part of Travis wanted to keep his mouth shut and toast the hard-earned signed contract while another part of him didn't think that would be right. Still, another fraction of his being urged him to accept Bella's offer and get out of this partnership before things got ugly.

"Okay, God," he said reclining in his chair and gazing at the ceiling. "Derek said we're supposed to come to You with everything? So. . .what do You think?"

Inhaling deeply, Travis wondered how long he'd have to wait for a Divine reply.

He glanced at his watch. Just after four. His stomach moaned in protest to eating only a chef's salad at lunchtime. Picking up the phone, Travis called his home number. Jena answered, and he could hear some kind of uproar in the background.

"Hi, Travis."

"Hi. What's going on over there?"

"Oh, your parents stopped by to see the kids, and Star came over just to say hello. She's got an important catering job tonight, and Rusty is going to help her."

"Good. Speaking of food, what's on the menu for tonight in the way of our dinner?"

"Well, fish, I think. Your dad brought over some rainbow

trout that he caught this morning. Now he's attempting to teach me how to clean the things, but it's totally grossing me out, and Star thinks it's hilarious."

Travis chuckled, imagining the scenario. "Listen, you happen to be speaking to the master chef of fried trout. I'll cook the fish, you make everything else."

"It's a deal."

"Great." Travis grinned. "Put my dad on the phone, okay?"

"Okay."

Several moments lapsed, then Travis heard the gravely voice of his father. At seventy years old, retired from a local foundry where he'd sweated away forty-plus years of his life, Reuben Larson now enjoyed his well-deserved free time. "Hello, Son."

"Hi. I understand you're traumatizing my summer girl."

A jolly guffaw filled the phone line. "Oh, a little fish guts won't scare her off. She works for you, doesn't she?"

"Touché." Amusement tugged at the corners of his mouth, and suddenly Travis longed to be there, visiting with his parents and teasing Jena. He wanted to tickle his daughters and laugh along with them. "Stay put, will you, Dad? I'm leaving the office right now."

"Okay, Mother and I will hang around and pester Jena a little while longer."

Disconnecting the call, Travis grabbed his suit coat and attaché case, locking his door on the way out.

"Hey, where are you running off to?" Craig asked as Travis passed his office. "I thought we had plans to go to The Black Tie."

"Another time."

"Well. . .all right. Josh, Yolanda, and I will be there if you change your mind."

"I won't, but have fun."

After a parting nod to the firm's secretary, Travis left the office suites of Duncan, Duncan, and Larson for that haven called home.

❧

The month of June sped by, and on the morning of July third, as she made a pot of coffee, Jena mulled over the comment Travis's mother had made only yesterday. *I haven't seen my son this happy since before Meg got sick. . .and it's all because of you.* While Jena knew she should feel flattered, she felt oddly unsettled. But maybe she was reading too much into Carol Larson's remark—and perhaps she was imagining those long looks that Travis often sent her way. Time and time again, Jena found him watching her, and it was all she could do not to feel nervous and self-conscious. What in the world could he be staring at?

Star, of course, had the answer. "He's crazy about you. Can't you tell? I can. . .and so can Rusty."

But Jena had trouble accepting that piece of logic, largely because she'd never known any man to be "crazy" about her. Except, she prayed for that very thing—a man to love her and one she could love right back.

Giggles and heavy footfalls on the steps signaled the Larson family's descent from the second floor. Within moments, Travis, wearing blue jeans and a red polo shirt, strode into the kitchen with Carly perched on his shoulders. Mandi skipped in behind him.

"Good morning."

She smiled. "Good morning, Travis." Grabbing Carly's foot, she gave it a gentle tug, and the three-year-old blew her a soupy kiss that drizzled into her daddy's dark hair.

He groaned, lifting her off his shoulders, and Jena laughed.

Mandi hugged her around the waist. "Know what, Miss Jena?"

"What?" She kissed the top of the girl's head.

"My daddy's face is very scratchy when he wakes up."

"Oh. . ." Jena tried not to react, but embarrassment soon engulfed her.

"Get over here and sit down, Mandi. Miss Jena doesn't want to hear about my face."

Her own was flaming at the present. She turned around and pressed the button on the coffeemaker so Travis wouldn't see.

"And my face is not that scratchy."

"Yes, it is, Daddy."

Mandi's matter-of-fact tone struck Jena's funny bone, and she was hard pressed to contain her mirth. Hearing Travis's approach only made things worse.

"I see you laughing." He gave her a playful nudge.

Jena swallowed the rest of her amusement. "Sorry, Mandi cracked me up."

"Yeah, she's been known to crack me up too." Leaning his back against the counter, Travis folded his arms, and while she put away the bag of coffee, Jena could feel the weight of his stare, although she couldn't get herself to meet his gaze. A heartbeat later, he reached over her and pulled down a box of cereal from the cupboard, giving Jena a generous whiff of his spicy aftershave. If she didn't know better, she could almost swear that he purposely tried to get her attention—just like when Jeff Sawyer used to pull her hair in the fifth grade because he had a crush on her. Maybe men weren't all that different from boys.

"So what's the plan for today?"

"The plan?"

His arm brushed against hers for the briefest of moments as he retrieved three bowls. "You mentioned something about a parade and a block party. . ."

Well, if my brain hadn't just turned to mush, I could tell you.

"Bella invited us to the top of her penthouse for the fireworks tonight. I told you about that, didn't I?"

"Um, yeah."

Jena suddenly felt like they were playing house. Travis was the daddy, and she was the mommy. . .

Oh, Lord, help! My thoughts are in a jumble.

"Everything okay, Jen?"

Travis stood beside her again, and this time he touched her shoulder. Jena didn't even try to avert her line of vision and looked full into his face. She allowed her gaze to roam over his clean-shaven jaw and nicely shaped mouth before her eyes met his. She thought she could drown in their deep brown depths. But then, she became aware of the tiny mar of concern that indented his dark brow. She forced a smile, and his frown disappeared.

"I'm fine," she reassured him. "I think I just need my morning cup of coffee."

eighteen

Jena glanced around the Minniatis' crowded penthouse. Bella really knew how to throw a bash. The kitchen, dining room, living room, and outdoor patio had been decorated in reds, whites, and blues, complete with streamers and balloons. Bella, herself, resembled an American flag as she mingled with her guests, most of whom were strapping young men. Jena presumed they represented the Mavericks indoor football team, and it appeared many had brought their wives and children along. In addition to a myriad of hors d'oeuvres and relish trays, the caterers served grilled tenderloin finger sandwiches. Jena thought it a shame that Star had already been booked for tonight, although she might not have been able accommodate this crowd.

"When are the fireworks gonna start?" Mandi wanted to know.

Jena looked at her wristwatch. Eight o'clock. "In about an hour."

Carly heaved a sigh. "That's a long time."

"Not that long," Mandi argued. "Besides, it has to be dark out first before we can see the fireworks, so Daddy said we get to stay up late."

Carly ceased her complaining.

Jena coaxed the girls out onto the rooftop patio. A panoramic view of Lake Michigan spread out before them. A few miles away, a summer festival drew throngs of people to the lakefront, and Jena pointed out the Ferris wheel and other brightly lit attractions.

"Can we go there?" Carly asked. "To the fair?"

"Maybe. But not tonight." Jena thought a weekday afternoon might be a good time to attend, and if she recalled correctly, the festival ran for the next five days.

"There you are!"

Glancing over her shoulder, Jena saw Bella Minniati heading their way, wearing a navy skirt and a red and white silk top. Travis followed close behind her.

"I've been looking everywhere for you! Great news." Bella paused just inches away, and Jena got a whiff of her expensive perfume. "Travis is coming to work for the Mavericks. Isn't that awesome? It's about time he ditched those crooks, Duncan and Duncan. Don't you agree?"

Jena swallowed a laugh. "No comment. I'm only the summer girl."

Travis let his head drop back and hooted. "Since when did that ever stop you from voicing your opinion?"

She gave him an indignant glare before looking at Bella and rolling her eyes.

"You know, you two are really cute together. But. . ." Bella waved a hand. ". . .don't count on me to play matchmaker. I initiated a relationship between a couple of my best friends, and once they got married, they never forgave me."

Jena laughed.

"Listen, Bella, the last thing Jena and I need is you playing matchmaker."

"Whatever you say, Travis." She turned to Jena. "Now, then, let's you and I talk some business."

"Bella, this is a party. You're supposed to relax and enjoy yourself."

"You hush."

He expelled an audible breath.

"Joe and I are purchasing a daycare center," Bella said, "and we'd like you to head it up—be its director."

"Me?" Jena could scarcely contain herself. Bella was offering her a dream come true! "When?"

"As soon as possible."

"Well, I, um, have to finish my last semester of college."

"Fine. Can you start January second?"

"Oh, well. . ."

Jena recalled her contract with Travis and what he'd said the afternoon before she'd signed it. With people like Bella Minniati in the world, we need a contract. Sliding her gaze to the right, Jena found him rocking on the soles of his feet as he stared out over at the lake with an ever-so-innocent expression plastered on his handsome face. That snake! He'd known what he was doing the entire time. But in rethinking the matter, Jena realized she couldn't feel angry with him. He paid her a great salary, and she lived rent-free.

"Actually, Bella, I wouldn't be able to start until June first of next year."

"Oh?" Bella looked at Travis. "And why is that?"

"I signed a contract promising to watch Mandi and Carly for the next year."

"You traitor!" Bella exclaimed with a toss of her blond head. "How could you?"

"I'm not a traitor. You gave me fair warning."

Jena couldn't help feeling rather flattered that Bella and Travis were fighting over her services. "Maybe we can come to some sort of compromise."

Travis gave her a terse look that said he wouldn't budge on the matter.

"On second thought, Bella, I think you're going to have to find yourself another director."

The slim, blond woman's face contorted in sheer aggravation. "Don't let him cow you, Jena. I'm sure there's a loophole in that contract somewhere."

"I doubt it, but it doesn't matter. Travis isn't cowing me. He's doing me a huge favor. I'm the one making out in this deal."

"Yeah, see, Bella?" Travis slipped an arm around Jena's shoulders. "I'm actually helping Jena out."

While that much was true, Jena couldn't help but wish she understood her boss. He didn't want Bella to play matchmaker, yet here he stood with his arm around her. Furthermore, he looked at her hard enough to make her knees weak. Was it just his way of being kind? She hadn't thought so this morning. . .

"I can't believe you went behind my back and did this, Travis, knowing I wanted to hire Jena. I don't suppose you told her about my offer before you convinced her to sign your contract."

"I didn't go behind your back. You said you were giving me fair warning about stealing my summer girl." Travis shrugged. "So I did something about it."

Travis's hand slipped from Jena's shoulder to the back of her neck where it felt like a branding iron against her skin. She held perfectly still, thinking he should remove it for propriety's sake but wishing he'd hold on to her forever.

"Listen, Bella, if you're looking to hire a spineless attorney, I'm not the guy. But I'm not a crook, either."

Bella pursed her lips and regarded him with a raised eyebrow. "Oh, you're right, Travis. I hate to admit it, but you're absolutely right. You played fair and square." She sighed and glanced at Jena. "Take a lesson from me. Keep your wits about you, or else you might find yourself working for Travis Larson for the rest of your natural-born days!"

"There are worse things in life, you know, Bella."

That's the truth, Jena thought with a grin. But before she could utter a syllable, her attention was captured by two little girls who couldn't wait for the sun to set.

Much later, on the way home after a spectacular display of

fireworks, Jena noted that Travis seemed unusually quiet. She didn't question him and instead listened as Mandi sang an interesting rendition of America the Beautiful. ". . .the land of the Braves and the home of the free."

Jena giggled inwardly. Travis was more influential on his daughters than she gave him credit. But as a very sports-minded male, she figured he'd do well as the Mavericks' lawyer.

They reached Travis's white stucco home, and while he carried Carly's sleeping form upstairs, Jena tended to Mandi. Before long, the girls were tucked into bed and on their way to a peaceful night's sleep.

"Hey, Jena. . ." Travis turned on the stairway, his right foot planted on the same step on which she stood, his other one step down. "I've been thinking. . .maybe I did bamboozle you into signing that contract. If you'd like, I'll let you out of it. The last thing I want is for you to be unhappy."

"I'm not unhappy. Not in the least."

"But you might be, come graduation time when that director's position looks a lot more rewarding than watching my daughters."

It occurred to Jena that Travis must have been brooding over this very issue since the show of fireworks began.

"Travis, the contract I signed with you works for me and my schedule. If Bella still needs a director in the spring, then. . .I'll let you negotiate that contract for me." She laughed.

He smiled. "You're sure?"

"Positive."

"Last chance."

She let it go. God showed her she'd done the right thing in agreeing to stay here for the next year. "Travis, did you hear what Mandi said to me tonight just before you turned off her bedroom lamp?"

"She said she loved you. She always says that. Carly too. That's why I hate the thought of you getting another job."

"And that's why I'm not ready to go. I don't mean to overstate my position here, but I believe the girls need me right now."

"Hardly an overstatement. They do need you. . .and so do I."

Jena's heart seemed to stop at his admission, although she reasoned that he could be referring to the stability factor in his life and in the lives of his girls. But when Travis reached out and brushed several strands of hair off her cheek, Jena had a hunch stability wasn't what he meant. His eyes darkened with emotion, and her mouth went dry. *He's going to kiss me!*

But in the next moment, the telephone rang and jangled them both back to their senses.

"I should go home. . ."

Travis nodded before bounding up the stairs to get the call. "G'night, Jen."

"Good night."

&

As the days progressed, Travis became engrossed with wrapping up his job at his law firm. Jena saw him for only minutes in the morning, and he rarely came home for dinner. She told herself she should feel relieved. No more long looks and emotionally charged interludes in the stairwell to deal with, but the truth was—Jena rather missed Travis. What's more, Mandi and Carly missed their daddy. But he phoned a couple of times each day, and the girls got a chance to chat with him.

Then, the month of August arrived, bringing with it a week's worth of thunderstorms. Jena took the girls everywhere she could think of just to keep from getting shack happy. They visited the museum, the art center, saw a silly movie with Star and Rusty, went roller-skating—after which Jena could barely walk. By the end of the week, all she wanted to do was relax at home and read a good book. However, Jena made one more trip—to the library, where she checked out several videos for Mandi and Carly and a novel for herself. Back home, she carried the television and VCR unit up from the basement playroom, rearranged the furniture in the living room, and made a tent for the girls with every blanket she could find upstairs. Finally, she lit a cozy fire in the fireplace and flopped onto the sofa with her story, *A Bride for the Pirate*. All was going well as the storm lit up the gloomy sky outside—

But then Travis came home unexpectedly at two in the afternoon.

"Hi, Daddy!"

Uh-oh. At Mandi's exclamation, Jena froze. She'd been so engrossed in her book that she hadn't heard him come in. Lying on her back, she had her stocking feet up on the arm of the sofa, and she hoped Travis wouldn't mind that she was lounging on the job and that his formal living room had been turned upside down. Slowly, she righted herself, combed her fingers through her hair, and stood.

"Hi, Travis." Jena thought he looked shocked as he surveyed the dismantled room. "I had planned to have this all cleaned up by the time you got home tonight."

He pursed his lips, nodded, but didn't say a word.

"We've got a tent, Daddy."

"So I see." Looking away from Mandi, he met Jena's gaze. "Something wrong with the TV room or the playroom downstairs?"

She grimaced. "No fireplace."

"Ah. . ."

Carly ran to him, and Travis scooped her up into his arms. "Wanna come inside our tent and watch *Mary Poppins* with us?"

"I won't fit in your tent, Baby." After hugging and kissing his youngest, he set her feet on the off-white carpet, straightened, and regarded Jena again. "But I'll tell you what I will do."

She gave him an expectant look and a tentative smile.

He loosened his tie. "I'm going to cancel my three-thirty appointment and pop some corn. I mean, Jena, really, how could you have forgotten the popcorn?"

He walked off before she could reply.

Jena gaped in his wake. Sitting back down on the couch, she tried to convince herself of how glad she felt that Travis wasn't miffed at her, but all the while, anticipation surged through her being at the thought of his joining their rainy day diversion.

Minutes later, the smell of hot, buttery popcorn filled the house, and Travis re-entered the living room carrying a large bowl of the salty snack. He'd shed his tie and rolled the sleeves of his starched white dress shirt to his elbows. Pausing by the tent, he scooped out a portion for Mandi and Carly to share, then he headed for the other side of the sofa. . .or so Jena presumed. But instead, Travis planted himself right beside her.

She couldn't curb the nervous laugh that escaped her.

"Popcorn?"

"No, thanks." She'd probably choke on it. Was he being overly friendly again, or was he trying to make a point?

He tossed a handful of popcorn into his mouth. "What are you reading?"

Before she could stop him, he'd reached across her and snatched the novel.

He raised an eyebrow. *"A Bride for the Pirate?* Jena! What kind of junk is this?"

With her cheeks flaming from embarrassment, she grabbed back her book. "It's not smut. It's an inspirational romance. The sardonic pirate realizes the error of his ways and gives all his ill-gotten gains to charity."

"And here I thought you were watching *Mary Poppins.*"

Jena laughed. She'd missed Travis's teasing. Then he stretched his arm out around the back of her shoulders, and she knew he wasn't just being overly friendly anymore.

She closed her eyes. "Travis, what are you doing?" When no reply came forth, she turned to look at him.

He met her questioning stare. "I'm falling for my summer girl, that's what I'm doing."

Jena glanced down at her hands, gripping the novel in her lap. She could scarcely believe the words Travis spoke—like something out of a beautiful love story.

"The truth is," he said, leaning closer, "I've been falling for you for months."

Her heart seemed to swell in her chest.

"Jena, say something, will you?"

"I can't. I think I just forgot how to breathe."

Hearing his laugh, she looked up at him.

"You're cute, know that?"

Moving his hand behind her head, Travis pulled her toward him and placed a gentle kiss on her lips. Jena's head began to swim in a pool of sheer pleasure that sent delicious tingles to her toes. She didn't want it to stop. As if sensing it, Travis kissed her again.

"Daddy. . . ?"

At the sound of Mandi's voice, Jena pulled back. She noted the stunned expression that crossed the little girl's face. But Travis didn't seem the least bit troubled and kept his arm around Jena.

"What is it, Honey?"

Mandi inched her way forward before breaking out in a huge grin. "You were kissing Miss Jena!"

"Yes, I was."

Mandi's steps quickened until she reached her father and climbed up into his lap. Travis handed the popcorn to Jena, and she set it on the floor.

"Do you like Miss Jena, Daddy?" The six-year-old glanced from one to the other.

"Yeah, I like her a lot."

"Do you like my Daddy, Miss Jena?"

"Sure I do. I wouldn't have let him kiss me if I didn't like him."

"Satisfied?" Travis poked his finger into Mandi's ribs, and she wiggled and giggled. This brought Carly over to join the fun.

After a tickle-fest, the front doorbell chimed. Both girls jumped off the couch and ran to answer it.

"Expecting someone?"

Jena shook her head. But it wasn't long before Bella Minniati's voice wafted through the foyer and into the living room.

"I suppose we should greet her."

"She'll find us. Don't worry." Travis sent Jena a sheepish grin. "She was the three-thirty appointment I cancelled."

"Nice going."

Travis laughed.

"Well, well, well," Bella said, entering the living room seconds later, "aren't you two a cozy sight."

"Look at our tent!" Carly cried as she dove inside.

"How fun!" Bella smiled, surveying the blankets suspended from the two armchairs.

"And my daddy was kissing Miss Jena," Mandi blurted before she too ducked into the tent.

"Kissing Miss Jena?" Bella raised a brow. "In the tent?"

Jena felt a blush creep up her cheeks and go straight to her hairline.

"No, he kissed her on the couch," Mandi informed their guest.

Bella chuckled. "Was that in your contract too, Travis?"

He snapped his fingers as if to say he'd forgotten to add that small benefit to their agreement.

Unable to stand the embarrassment a moment longer, Jena stood. "Bella, would you like a cup of coffee?"

"I'd love one."

"Travis?"

"No, thanks."

Walking into the kitchen, Jena took her time preparing the rich-smelling brew. The scene with Travis played over and over in her mind. She felt his kiss on her lips and heard the words he'd said: "I think I'm falling for my summer girl."

Oh, Lord, she silently prayed, *help me out here. I think I'm falling for Travis too!*

nineteen

Bella stayed for dinner since Joe had to work late that night. She chattered on about her pregnancy and the daycare center. "We're closing on the building next Friday," she said. "I'll be interviewing for a director sometime after that. I think most of the staff can stay, but I really want someone with Christian values running the place."

Jena felt the weight of Bella's stare. But she occupied herself with tending to Carly and making sure the little one got more food inside of her than on the floor. As tempting as the director's position sounded, Jena had made her decision. However, she couldn't help wondering if or how things would change since she and Travis had admitted their fondness for each other.

Once they'd finished their meal, Bella helped Jena clear the table. Shortly thereafter, Star and Rusty stopped by to say hello. The rain had dissipated and the dark clouds broke, allowing slivers of sunshine through. When seven-thirty rolled around, the girls kicked up a fuss and didn't want to go to bed, so Jena opted to take them for a walk. After all, the children had been cooped up practically all week. Everyone went along, Bella, Star, Rusty, and Travis.

Ambling along on the sidewalk, heading for Lake Drive, Travis sat Carly on his shoulders while, up ahead, Mandi rode her bike. Jena strolled in between Bella and Star, but the two carried on like magpies, so she stepped back and listened to Travis and Rusty discuss sports scores. The group stopped at the top of Atwater Beach to let the girls climb on the play equipment. Then they began their trek back by way of Capitol Drive.

Arriving home, Jena realized the girls needed baths. They had somehow managed to rove over mud puddles. One by one, the guests bid their adieus and went their separate ways. Jena had just gotten Carly into her nightie when Travis came upstairs. The girls soon talked him into reading them a book, so Jena took advantage of the time and cleaned up the kitchen—even though she was technically done for the day. But, oddly, the lines of duty now blurred. That kiss this afternoon had changed everything as far as Jena was concerned. She only wished Travis would come downstairs so they could talk about it. About them. Had it meant more to her than to him? What was he thinking?

What was she thinking?

Oh, Lord, I haven't had time to pray about this situation.

With the kitchen cleaned and still no sign of Travis, Jena meandered across the yard and up to her apartment. She kicked off her shoes, turned on lights, and checked the phone's answering machine for messages. She picked through her mail, opening an envelope with her college's emblem on the upper left hand corner. To her delight, it was her final class schedule. School began in just three short weeks. . .

The phone rang, and Jena picked up the call.

"Hey, what about this living room? It's a disaster."

Jena winced. "Oh, sorry, Travis. I forgot all about it. I'll be right over."

She hung up the phone and raced downstairs and across the courtyard. All the while, she thought Travis sounded like her employer again.

Lord, You know I'm naïve when it comes to men. If Travis is falling for me, what's my position here? How do I define it, and when do I act like his employee and when do I act like his friend. . .are we even friends?

Jena sighed, feeling baffled. Entering the living room, she pulled a blanket off one of the armchairs and began folding it when Travis caught her around the midsection. A startled gasp escaped her lips, and she dropped the blanket.

"Forget about cleaning up." His warm breath sent shivers down her spine. "I've got other things on my mind."

"Um, Travis. . ."

He began to kiss her neck, and while Jena enjoyed reading about handsome heroes sweeping women off their feet, she suddenly panicked, thinking she might have walked into a situation she couldn't handle.

She turned in his arms, and he kissed the protest from her lips. She felt like giving up and drowning in his ardor but knew she could not. At last she came up for air and managed to mutter the word, "STOP!" as he trailed kisses across her cheek and down her neck.

"Travis, please stop. Please!"

He brought his chin back, and Jena noted the surprise in his dark brown eyes. With her hands on his chest, she tried in vain to create some distance between them. She felt like sobbing. She felt cheap.

"You're going way too fast for me," she managed.

He looked full into her face and seemed to wrestle with his emotions. "My apologies. I thought the feeling was mutual."

"It is, but you're going to have to take things slowly with me. I'm. . .well, I'm really stupid when it comes to. . .you know, this kind of stuff."

He narrowed his gaze while an expression of disbelief crossed his features. "What are you telling me, Jena? That you're twenty-six and you've never—"

"No, I've never! My chastity belongs to the Lord until I get married!"

Travis appeared all the more shocked. "I didn't mean it that way. I wasn't about to. . .well, you know. . ."

She pressed her lips together, trying to stave off the threatening tears, but they leaked from her eyes despite her best efforts.

She lowered her chin. "I. . .I'm sorry. . ."

He exhaled, and his breath was like a whisper across her cheek. "Don't cry, Jena, and there's nothing to be sorry about." He gathered her in his arms but held her in a much different way. "I'm the one behaving like a. . .pirate."

She laughed through her tears. "Not at all." Resting her chin against his shoulder, she wiped the moisture from her eyes. Had Travis been less than the gentleman he was, she might have gotten into some serious trouble. "But I really didn't mean to lead you on."

"You didn't lead me on. I mean, I know you're not that kind of a woman. But at the same time, I didn't think a little fooling around would hurt anything."

Jena suddenly longed to make Travis understand her views—God's views. "I don't believe a man should touch a woman like that unless she belongs to him in marriage. I should have said something earlier this afternoon. But the truth is, I was sort of in shock when you kissed me on the couch, and I. . .well, I liked it."

A hint of a grin curled one side of Travis's mouth.

"But that doesn't mean it was right. I understand that physical intimacy between two people who are attracted to each other is just expected in this world. But, Travis, you and I aren't of the world anymore. We're Christians."

He narrowed his gaze, thinking over her reply. "Okay. Point taken," he said, allowing his arms to fall from around her waist. "I see what you mean."

"I'm so glad." Jena took a step back.

"I promise to behave myself from here on in."

She regarded him askance. "As my employer?"

Travis blinked, looking confused. "Well, yes. . .although I would like to be more than just your employer." He cocked his head. "What do you want?"

Jena smiled. "I want what God wants. If He has ordained a union between you and me, He'll show us as we walk with Him day by day and step by step."

Travis pursed his lips in his habitual manner. She knew right then that he'd taken her comments to heart.

"I think you're very charming." Jena felt her face warm as she spoke, but she couldn't seem to help what she said. The words glided off her tongue in all honesty.

His face brightened. "Why, thank you. That's the nicest thing anyone's said to me all day."

She laughed, and he pulled another fuzzy throw off the chair. "What do you say we clean up this living room?"

After a nod, she followed his lead and picked up the blanket she'd discarded only minutes before.

☙

Weeks later, Travis stared out the window of his new office. He had a decent view from this downtown high-rise, unlike the one he'd occupied at D D & L—make that D D & T now that Yolanda Timmerman moved into a partnership there. The career move had proven to be a good one for him. Travis felt glad he'd made the right decision. But if it hadn't been for Jena, he probably wouldn't have had the courage or confidence to leave the firm. God brought her into his life at just the perfect time.

Grinning to himself, Travis thought over the candlelit dinner they shared last night in celebration of her birthday. Star prepared their meal, and Rusty waited on them, as he and Jena sat at his formally set dining room table. Forget any romance; Travis never laughed so hard in his life. He was only too glad he didn't have to pay the wisecracking cook or tip their clumsy waiter.

Chuckling at the memory, he never imagined he'd have so much fun courting a woman with old-fashioned values—or as Derek Ryan put it, "biblical standards." Travis found it refreshing. What a relief to know Jena didn't adhere to the popular culture. She reminded Travis of Meg—but that, and their faith, was as far as the similarities went. Jena was her own person, and the more Travis got to know her, the more he grew to love her. Mandi and Carly adored her. His parents liked and respected her. . .

What am I waiting for? Why don't I ask her to marry me? She'd say yes. I can see it in her eyes. . .

"Travis Larson?"

"Hmm?" He whirled around to find a broad-shouldered young man standing in his doorway.

"I'm Bernie Thomas. Isabella Minniati sent me over to discuss some of the terms in my contract. My agent will be here in a few minutes."

"Great." Travis smiled and stuck out his right hand. The other man shook it. "Nice to meet you. Have a seat, Bernie."

❧

Jena looked up at the sky and decided she'd never seen so many stars. They sparkled like diamonds against black velvet.

"Jen?"

She turned to Travis who sat in an adjacent lawn chair, his feet up on a white, wrought-iron table.

"It's ninety degrees out at ten o'clock at night. How can you be drinking hot coffee?"

She laughed and glanced down at the cup in her hand. "It's a terrible habit. I should quit it. But after all the years of going to school during the day and working at night—or vice versa—then doing homework in the wee hours of the morning, I got used to living on caffeine."

"This semester ought to be easier for you."

"It's going to be a piece of cake, and I have you to thank for that."

"It works both ways, Jen."

She smiled. He sure was handsome, sitting there in the courtyard under the moonlight.

"So, are you still praying about marrying a man in the ministry?"

Jena frowned. "What?"

Travis chuckled. "Never mind. I guess there's my answer."

She rolled her eyes and looked back up into the sky. *I'm praying about marrying you, Silly,* she wanted to say. But she couldn't bring herself to be quite so audacious. Having seen Travis interact with Star and Bella, she sensed that he didn't care for bold and overconfident women, although he could hold his own around them. Jena had seen that too.

She heard him slap at a mosquito. "Got any special plans for Saturday?"

Jena thought it over. Two days from now. . .

"No, not that I can recall right off the top of my head."

"Well, pencil me into your agenda. We're going to do something special. I don't know what yet, but you, me, and the girls will have a great time."

"Okay."

Travis stood. "I hate to do this, but I'm going in. The bugs are almost as bad as the humidity. You're welcome to join me. We can watch a movie or something."

Jena was tempted—very tempted. She knew Travis would behave like a complete gentleman, and she'd like nothing more than to spend extra time with him. But she had been trying to find a couple of hours all day in which to sit down and pay her bills and fold her clean laundry. "Oh, I guess I'll call it a night. I have things I should probably accomplish by tomorrow."

"Okay, then I'll walk you home."

She laughed. The distance was probably twenty feet or less.

Travis held out his hand. Jena took it, and he pulled her to her feet. At her apartment door, he placed a chaste kiss on her cheek.

"Night, Jen."

"Good night, Travis."

She walked inside, latched the door behind her, then climbed the narrow staircase to her apartment. She turned on the television and listened to tail end of the nightly newscast as she began her chores.

By midnight, she crawled into bed, and just when she began to doze, she thought she heard the downstairs door open and slam shut. Sitting up in bed her heart raced in fear as she heard footfalls ascending the steps. They sounded too light and quick to belong to Travis or any other man. Next, she heard keys jangle as the top door was unlocked and opened. It, too, was forcefully closed as if pushed with a foot.

Curiosity replaced her panic, and Jena slipped out of bed. She grabbed her robe and slipped it on. A thunk sounded, once, twice, as if someone dropped a heavy box or luggage— or both—on the living room floor. From the doorway of her bedroom, she saw a light go on. With slow, measured steps, Jena made her way toward the intruder. Pausing in the dining room, she thought she recognized the slender woman whose sandy-brown hair was swept up off her neck. She'd seen her photograph around Travis's house.

The woman turned and shrieked when she spotted Jena. "Oh!" she exclaimed, covering the left side of her chest. "Oh, you nearly gave me a heart attack."

"You scared me half to death too."

The woman narrowed her gaze, a trait Jena knew so well. "Who are you, and what are you doing here?"

"My name is Jena Calhoun. Travis hired me to take care of Mandi and Carly this summer." She smiled. "You must be his sister, Glenda."

"You're very astute, aren't you? Well, that's good. You'll be able to find another job in no time." Glenda collapsed into the couch. "My flight at O'Hare got cancelled, and I was forced to take the bus from Chicago to Milwaukee. But I'm back now, so first thing tomorrow morning you can pack your things and leave."

Jena didn't reply as questions flittered through her mind. Hadn't Glenda left to get married? Where was her husband? Did Travis know his sister had come back? Probably not!

Padding back to the bedroom, Jena closed the door without a sound. Next, she picked up the phone and pressed number one of the speed dial feature.

"Yeah, hello. . ."

"Travis, it's Jena. Sorry to wake you, but, um. . .we've got a little problem here. . ."

twenty

"I can't believe you're taking her side over mine."

Travis turned from his office window where he'd been watching Jena and the girls walk up Shorewood Boulevard, heading to the high school for Mandi's morning swimming lesson. He glared at his sister. "You've got a lot of nerve showing up and making demands."

"Travis, I'm your sister."

"Doesn't matter. You happen to be interrupting a very delightful romance between Jena and me."

Glenda expelled a sigh of disgust. "Oh, Travis, she is so totally not your type."

"That just proves how little you know of the situation. . . and of Jena and me."

Glenda stepped towards him. "Travis, I have nowhere else to go."

"Then you'll have to move in with Mom and Dad."

"Are you out of your mind? I can't call them!" Glenda's face contorted with indignation. "They haven't forgiven me for eloping with Scott."

"Months ago, I would have said I hadn't forgiven you either. But the truth is, your leaving was the best thing that happened to me."

"Oh, thanks a lot."

He grinned at the quip. "So what happened with Scott?"

"He's a loser, that's what happened."

Travis chewed the corner of his lower lip and folded his arms as he contemplated Glenda's remark. Scott Jenkins never appeared to be a "loser" while he'd been Travis's assistant for eighteen months at D D & L. "What constitutes a loser?"

"A man who can't even bring in a salary that'll support his. . . family. That's a loser."

"What, did Scott tell you to get a job or something?"

"Or something," came her vague reply.

Travis digested the news. The situation didn't seem so bad after all. Glenda would come to her senses and go back to Scott in a day or two. In the meantime, she could continue to sleep in Mandi's room while his daughters shared Carly's bed.

"Travis, I think our arrangement worked out great, and that's why I want things to be the way they used to be."

"That was another lifetime ago. Our arrangement doesn't exist anymore. I don't know how to explain it exactly, but I feel like a completely different person." He paused and wondered about divulging his secret, then decided Glenda might as well know. "I'm also planning to ask Jena to marry me tomorrow." Travis rubbed his palms together. "I'm going to take her to the mall and stop in front of Rush's House of Diamonds, propose, and let her pick out her own engagement ring. Of course, I'll have to tease her a little bit first. That'll be half the fun."

"Travis, you're off your rocker."

"Yeah, but I'm happy, the girls are happy, Jena's happy. . .so who cares?"

Glenda rolled her brown eyes. "Take it from your little sister. Stay single. Play the field."

"I don't want to play the field. I want Jena. Besides, I've been married before, and I was happy then too."

"Which raises another question. How can you disregard Meg's memory by remarrying someone like that. . .that—"

"Watch it." He pointed a finger at her. "You're treading on very dangerous ground right now. As for my remarrying, Meg would want me to be happy, and she'd like Jena."

Travis walked out of his office and into the kitchen where he poured himself a cup of coffee. Glancing at the clock above the kitchen sink, he realized he had to leave soon in order to make his ten o'clock appointment. He had a full day ahead and no time for his sister's antics. But one thing seemed sure: Glenda couldn't stay here and harass Jena all day.

She came up behind him as he twisted on the top of his travel mug.

"Travis, I helped you out when you were in a bind. I practically raised Mandi and Carly. They're like my own children. Carly was a newborn when Meg died, and—"

"And I appreciate everything you did for me and the girls, okay? But things are different now." He expelled a weary breath. "Look, Jena said she didn't need the Volvo today. Take the car and go visit Mom and Dad. Tonight you can sleep in Mandi's room again."

"Travis, that's only temporary. I need a residence that's. . . well, more permanent."

He raised a brow. "Why?"

Glenda tore her gaze away from him and tears filled her eyes. "Because Scott's already filed for divorce, and I'm going to have a baby."

"What?" He felt his jaw go slack before he shook his head. "Oh, man. . ."

"I have nowhere else to go, Trav."

"Okay, okay. . ." He held up a hand to forestall the giant pity party he sensed was coming. Leave it to his sister to dump a crisis on him just as he had to take off for work. "Glenda, I want you to go visit Mom today. The two of you need to talk. I'll try to get home early this afternoon, and we can discuss your situation further, all right?"

She shrugged and swatted at an errant tear.

Moving forward, Travis kissed his sister's cheek and gave her a quick hug. "Relax. Everything'll be okay. Try not to worry, all right?"

Again, she merely shrugged, and as he left the house, Travis prayed he'd be able to take his own advice.

❧

Jena arrived back home at noon to find Travis's sister on the phone and watching a daytime drama in the den. Jena kept the girls in the kitchen while she put together one of their favorite lunches—peanut butter and jelly sandwiches and sliced apples. But even keeping her distance, Jena couldn't help over-hearing snippets of Glenda's conversation—mainly because the woman hollered every other word. Soon, Jena put the facts together: Glenda's marriage didn't work out, she was pregnant, and her parents didn't want her moving in with them.

Oh, Lord, this woman needs to know You so desperately. . .

When Glenda sauntered into the kitchen, looking as though she'd been crying, Jena tried to reach out to her.

"Can I make you some lunch?"

"No. Thanks."

"I'm available if you need somebody to talk to."

"I don't." She knelt down in between her nieces' chairs. "How about we go to the movies this afternoon? You two and me. . .just like old times."

Both girls smiled.

"Can Miss Jena come too?" Mandi asked.

"No, this is just for Aunty Glenda and her girls. I haven't seen you in so long, and I've missed you. That's why I came back."

Mandi glanced over her shoulder and gave Jena a worried look. "But, Miss Jena takes care of us now."

"Don't you want me taking care of you anymore? Remember how much fun we used to have?"

Jena suddenly felt like a lioness who wanted to defend her

cubs. "Glenda, that's unfair to put Mandi and Carly in such a terrible position. They're children. They don't want to decide between you and me. Besides, it's not their decision to make. Let Travis handle it."

If the glare that Glenda hurled her way had been a stone, Jena would have dropped dead from the impact. "Stay out of it. This is a family affair." She turned back to the girls. "Come on. Let's go see a movie."

Glenda took hold of the girls' forearms and practically dragged them off their seats.

"My samich!" Carly cried, stomping her feet.

Jena put a hand over her mouth to keep from saying something she'd regret. Carly was tired. She needed a nap.

Glenda grabbed the food off the plate and handed it to the three-year-old. "Here. Eat it on the way."

Mandi glanced at Jena with uncertainty pooling in her eyes.

Jena tamped down her own disquiet and smiled at Mandi. "It'll be okay, Precious." Gazing over the girl's head, she saw Glenda heading for the back door. "Hey, wait a sec!"

The woman turned around. "Now what?"

"Do you think it might be wise to call Travis and let him know you're taking the girls?"

Glenda laughed. "I don't have to pester my brother at work for such a trivial matter. I practically raised these children. But you've been here, what. . .three months?" A little sneer curved her perfectly shaped lips. "If you feel you need to call, go ahead. Travis knows my cell phone number. If there's some problem, he can call me. But there won't be."

Jena didn't have a reply. She didn't know enough about the situation to give one. Moreover, she had no idea what Travis told his sister this morning. Maybe he consented to the movie.

With every muscle in her body tense with protest, Jena watched Glenda leave with the girls. Next, she walked to the phone. She didn't care if the matter was "trivial," she wanted Travis to know about it. Besides, he never cared when she phoned him at work.

Her hands trembled as she punched in his number. But her heart sank when the receptionist said he was out of the office. Jena tried his mobile phone but got his voice mail. She decided to leave a message. "Travis, it's Jena. I just thought I'd let you know your sister. . ." She paused to clear the emotion from her throat. ". . .your sister took the girls to a movie this afternoon. She said if there was a problem, you could call her cell phone. She said you knew the number. See you later. . ."

Jena hung up and found that she felt so upset she shook like a leaf in an autumn wind. It occurred to her then that she hadn't just fallen in love with Travis—but with his daughters too.

A hard knocking at the back door caused her to jump.

"Jena? Jena, are you there?"

"Yes, come in, Mrs. Barlow."

The white-haired lady stepped inside the house and smiled. She wore a navy floral housedress and on her feet were canvas slip-ons. "I don't mean to be nosy, Dear, but was that Glenda Larson pulling away with the girls in the car?"

Jena nodded. . .and then she just couldn't help it. She burst into tears and blurted out the whole sordid mess.

"And now she wants her apartment and her job back. . ."

Mrs. Barlow pulled Jena into her capable tan arms. "There, there, you know as well as I do that Travis isn't about to let that happen. He loves you, Jena."

"I love him too."

"I can tell. It's been so exciting to watch your relationship bloom like my gladiolas!"

Jena had to laugh at the analogy, then stepped back and wiped away her tears. "Mrs. Barlow, it's amazing. . .my mother is so excited. She called me twice this week to ask if Travis 'popped the question yet.'"

The older woman chuckled. "That's what God can do. He can repair and restore."

Jena agreed, but then a cloud of gloom overshadowed her burst of joy. "But what about Glenda? What about this situation? I feel like she hates me."

"Well, I do have a suggestion. I don't know if you'll like it, but. . ."

"Let's hear it." Jena peered into the woman's age-lined face. "You're the one who got me the job here. Maybe God will use you in this predicament with Travis's sister too."

❧

Travis listened to Jena's message. Hearing the strained tone in her voice, he knew she was upset. He tried to call her back, but there wasn't any answer at home. When he got ahold of Glenda, he gave her a tongue-lashing, not that it made a difference to his selfish sister. Then, all afternoon, he tried to wrap things up and get home, but the more he attempted to speed things along, the more complications arose. But at last, he pulled into his driveway shortly after five o'clock. By phone, he had discovered Glenda and the girls were home, but Jena was still unaccounted for, much to Travis's dismay. He made a mental note to buy her a cell phone at the mall tomorrow—along with an engagement ring.

He walked into the small courtyard and immediately knew things were wrong. Toys had been thrown everywhere. Through an open window upstairs, he heard Carly bawling at the top of her lungs. It was a wonder the neighbors hadn't summoned the cops; the kid sounded like she was being tortured.

Entering the house, Travis made his way into the kitchen and saw the sink of cups and plastic plates. He placed his attaché on the table and realized too late that he'd set it in a gob of ketchup. A curse surfaced, but Travis gulped it back down.

Lord, I can't handle this. You know I can't handle this. I lived like this for three years, and I cannot—will not—go back.

Mandi ran into the kitchen, her face red and blotchy, tears streaming from her brown eyes. "Daddy," she sobbed, "Miss. . . Jena's. . .gone."

At that moment, Travis didn't know if he should panic over what his daughter said or the fact that she was about to hyperventilate.

"Mandi, calm down." He lifted her into his arms, and she clung to him, crying in a way that made melodramatics seem calm and rational. "Shh, Mandi, it's okay. Don't cry."

Glenda appeared in the doorway. "You know, Travis, these girls are out of control. I mean, I'm gone for just three months and look what that summer girl has done to them."

Travis felt his blood pressure hit the ceiling. "Glenda, it's a good thing I've got Mandi in my arms right now or I might be tempted to—"

"Oh, please! Spare me your idle threats." Her face scrunched up into a mask of resentment. "And after all I've done for you!"

"Where's Jena?"

"Don't ask me. She was gone when we came home from the movies."

"See. . .Daddy? Sh-she's gone," Mandi whimpered.

Travis shook his head. "She's not really gone. She's probably just at the store or something."

"Sorry to be the one to tell you this, Trav, but she packed up her stuff in the apartment, bedding, and everything. She's gone."

"What were you doing in Jena's apartment?"

"Don't yell at me! The girls were looking for her." Glenda threw her hands in the air. "I'm always the bad guy. Mom does the same thing. Everything that goes wrong in life gets blamed on me."

Travis watched his sister stomp off, and he felt like his life was spinning out of control. But somehow, his common sense managed to surface through the tumult. He knew Jena as well as he knew anyone. She wouldn't just pack up and move out without saying something to him.

"Mandi, stop crying," he said, setting his daughter down. "Miss Jena is not gone. I promise you she isn't. I don't know where she is right now, but she'll be back, okay? I promise."

The little girl nodded, and her sobs began to subside.

Travis stood and placed his hands on his hips, squeezing back his shoulder blades in an effort to ease his stress. He became aware of Carly's temper fit, still in progress, and debated whether he should go up there and see if he could settle her down or let her scream it out. But at that very instant, Jena came strolling into the courtyard carrying an overfilled laundry basket.

"Mandi." He grinned. "Miss Jena's back."

His daughter's eyes widened, and she ran for the back door. Travis followed her outside. Seeing him, Jena smiled, but then her eyebrows dipped into a frown as she glanced at the second floor.

"Oh, poor Carly. I knew she needed a nap today."

Mandi threw her arms around Jena's waist, nearly knocking her backwards. Travis caught Jena's elbow, steadied her, and then took the basket.

"Want to tell me what's going on?"

She gave Mandi a little hug and kissed the top of her head. "Let me take care of Carly and then. . .Travis, I have to talk to you about something."

His eyes widened with the obvious. "Yeah, I'd say so."

"Will you take the clean laundry up to the apartment for me?"

He nodded as Jena ran into the house. Looking at Mandi, Travis inclined his head toward the apartment door. "C'mon, you can help me."

For the first time since he'd come home that day, he saw his daughter smile.

❧

After rocking Carly to sleep, Jena made her way across the yard to the apartment she once called home. She couldn't wait to tell Travis about Mrs. Barlow's wonderful idea. It solved everything. What's more, as the afternoon progressed, Jena had become more and more burdened for Glenda. The woman obviously had emotional wounds that ran deep, and Jena prayed for the chance to tell Glenda about the Great Physician.

She climbed the stairs and entered the living room where she found Travis and Mandi sitting on the couch, the six-year-old nestled against her daddy's chest.

Jena smiled. "What a sweet picture. I wish I had my camera handy."

"Hmm. . .I'm anxious to hear why it isn't handy. From the looks of this place, you've moved out."

Jena lost her grin. "That's what I wanted to talk to you about."

"I figured." He sat up and plucked Mandi from his lap. "Go play for a while I talk to Miss Jena, okay?"

"Okay."

Mandi strode toward the door but paused beside Jena and gave her another hug. Jena returned the show of affection, and the child continued on her way.

Travis stepped forward and gathered Jena into his arms. He held her as if she'd been away for six months, and they were just now reunited. When he pulled back, she saw that his brown eyes had grown misty. "You're moving right back in here, Jena. I'm not letting you go."

"I don't want you to let me go—and I'm not going, except to Mrs. Barlow's house. I moved in with her. Temporarily."

Travis raised his brows. "You moved in with Mrs. Barlow?"

Jena nodded. "I want to win your sister over. I want to be her friend. I want to show her the love of Christ. She needs to know His love. That's why I think Glenda should have her apartment back."

"Great sentiments, Jen, but this place will be too small once her baby arrives."

"But that's six months from now, and by then, she and her husband could be back together, and you and I—"

Jena halted in mid-sentence. She couldn't believe her blunder.

"And you and I. . .what?" Travis had the nerve to smirk.

She felt her face begin to flame. "I think I, um, forgot what I was going to say."

"Oh, sure you did. Know what I think?"

She didn't reply, but the heat of her embarrassment spread to her neck and ears.

"I think you've been reading too many of those bride stories and wedding magazines."

Chagrined, she looked away and stared at an imaginary spot on the wall until Travis took hold of her chin and urged her gaze back to his. All traces of humor disappeared from his face.

"I love you, Jena."

"I love you too."

"Know what else I think?" He touched her lips with his and murmured, "I think you're going to make a beautiful bride. . ."

epilogue

Emerald green and white silk flowers, arranged in graceful swags, lined the end of each pew all the way to the altar. After earning her degree and graduating from college only two weeks ago, Jena now stood in the back of the church in preparation to meet her groom.

She watched Star glide down the center aisle. Mandi and Carly, dressed in frilly white dresses, seemed to float just behind her. Jena still couldn't believe she had put this wedding together in less than four months. Then, again, it wouldn't have been possible without Mrs. Barlow and Glenda's help. It had taken a while for her future sister-in-law to warm up, but by the time the leaves had turned to their autumn colors, Jena and Glenda had become friends. Shortly thereafter, Bella Minniati offered her a part-time job at her daycare center, which Glenda accepted. Under Bella's influence, her attitude improved, and Jena suspected it wouldn't be long before Glenda "came to Christ." Glenda's husband, Scott, noticed a positive difference in her and halted divorce proceedings. He even showed up today to see Travis get married.

Suddenly, Mr. Zuttle, the organist, began to play the bridal march, and Jena experienced a sudden attack of nerves. As if sensing it, her father gave her hand a reassuring squeeze before threading it around his elbow. Their procession began.

Up ahead, Jena glimpsed Travis, decked out in his black tuxedo. He looked so handsome that she could scarcely take her eyes off him. With cameras flashing on either side, she was only vaguely aware of passing her friends, relatives, and church family.

Reaching the altar, Jena's father handed her to Travis. He smiled into her eyes before looking at the pastor who stood poised and ready to perform the ceremony. Star, the maid of honor, adjusted Jena's lacy veil and the gown's elegant train, while Jena's brother, acting as the best man, grinned nearby. Jena had wanted more bridesmaids, including Glenda and Bella but both women were great with child. Then, with the time constraint, it had seemed much simpler to coordinate two people rather than an entire wedding party.

Thank You, Lord, that my family made the time to be with me here today. Maybe this wedding will bring us closer together. . .

"Who gives this woman to this man?" the pastor asked.

"I do, her father," Jena heard her dad say, just as he'd rehearsed the night before.

Smiling, she clung to Travis as her heart swelled with love. She'd never felt so happy in all her life. Who would have ever thought that an interim summer job would become her life-long career?

A Letter To Our Readers

Dear Reader:

In order that we might better contribute to your reading enjoyment, we would appreciate your taking a few minutes to respond to the following questions. We welcome your comments and read each form and letter we receive. When completed, please return to the following:

Fiction Editor
Heartsong Presents
PO Box 719
Uhrichsville, Ohio 44683

1. Did you enjoy reading *The Summer Girl* by Andrea Boeshaar?
   ❑ Very much! I would like to see more books by this author!
   ❑ Moderately. I would have enjoyed it more if

   _____

   _____

   _____

2. Are you a member of **Heartsong Presents**? ❑ Yes ❑ No
   If no, where did you purchase this book? _____

   _____

3. How would you rate, on a scale from 1 (poor) to 5 (superior), the cover design? _____

4. On a scale from 1 (poor) to 10 (superior), please rate the following elements.

   ____ Heroine   ____ Plot
   ____ Hero   ____ Inspirational theme
   ____ Setting   ____ Secondary characters

5. These characters were special because?_____

_____

_____

6. How has this book inspired your life?_____

_____

_____

7. What settings would you like to see covered in future
   Heartsong Presents books? _____

_____

_____

8. What are some inspirational themes you would like to see
   treated in future books? _____

_____

_____

9. Would you be interested in reading other **Heartsong
   Presents** titles? ❏ Yes   ❏ No

10. Please check your age range:
   ❏ Under 18   ❏ 18-24
   ❏ 25-34   ❏ 35-45
   ❏ 46-55   ❏ Over 55

Name_____
Occupation _____
Address _____
City_____ State_____ Zip_____

BROKEN THINGS

*F*avorite **Heartsong Presents** author Andrea Boeshaar takes us into the world of a woman who courageously faces the failure of her past when she finds a faded photograph of the Chicago cop she once loved. . .but left.

Fiction • 352 pages • 5 ³/₁₆" x 8"

❤ ❤ ❤ ❤ ❤ ❤ ❤ ❤ ❤ ❤ ❤ ❤

Heartsong

Presents

Great Inspirational Romance at a Great Price!

Heartsong Presents books are inspirational romances in contemporary and historical settings, designed to give you an enjoyable, spirit-lifting reading experience. You can choose wonderfully written titles from some of today's best authors like Hannah Alexander, Andrea Boeshaar, Yvonne Lehman, Tracie Peterson, and many others.

When ordering quantities less than twelve, above titles are $3.25 each.
Not all titles may be available at time of order.